PRAISE FOR *Fiddle*

"A fine swan song: a great plot and realistic hard-boiled-detective dialogue."
—*Playboy*

"Ed McBain's legion of loyal readers will reach the last pages of *Fiddlers* lost in their customary admiration for the prodigious skills so amply displayed . . . [McBain] closed out the 87th Precinct series on a characteristically high note. All of the qualities that made McBain special and lifted him so far above the genre he did so much to shape are here in abundance . . . The policeman's lot may not be a happy one, but readers of this triumphant culmination of the series . . . should be much cheered."
—*The Philadelphia Inquirer*

"McBain's final novel boasts all of the virtues we have come to expect from him: ingenious plotting, deft dialogue, engaging cynicism and, above all, credible characterization . . . [McBain] departs still at the top of his game and, like every great entertainer, leaving us both satisfied and hungry for more."
—*The San Diego Union-Tribune*

"There is an elegant symmetry to McBain's last dance, which times its steps to 'the brilliant fiddlers of the 87th Squad' whose tightly choreographed criminal investigations do indeed follow a musical structure . . . When the music stops and the band packs up, everyone is still on the floor—dancing."
—*The New York Times Book Review*

"McBain's handling of dialogue is superb and his wit as sharp as ever in this last book in the series that established the standard for ensemble procedurals." —*Alfred Hitchcock Mystery Magazine*

"With his vivid style, wit, sense of place and top-drawer dialogue, McBain takes the reader along as the 87th detectives identify pieces of the puzzle and put them in place . . . *Fiddlers* will satisfy longtime readers and should send first-timers to bookshops for the other fifty-four." —*San Antonio Express News*

"A fittingly engrossing finale for an author who proved as talented as anyone writing novels today." —*Omaha World Herald*

"By turns ribald, gritty and cynical . . . Nobody, but nobody, could weave the disparate details together like Ed McBain."
—*BookPage*

"At once startling and convincing . . . Even the briefest passing character comes across with a living, breathing individuality that fairly jumps off the page." —*Pittsburgh Post-Gazette*

"McBain's crime novels have also set the standard for excellence in the police procedural genre, and the author will forever retain his place in the mystery pantheon; *Fiddlers* makes a fitting final legacy. Highly recommended." —*Library Journal* (starred review)

"His 87th Precinct novels remain the benchmark for both police procedurals and crime series fiction. McBain just keeps getting better and better. This one will have readers waking in the middle of the night wondering if they, too, have killers inside themselves." —*Booklist* (starred and boxed)

"A single-plot mystery that feels far more generous, and one of the most comprehensive portraits of McBain's fictional kingdom of Isola ever." —*Kirkus Reviews*

Fiddlers

Also by Ed McBain

The 87th Precinct Novels

Cop Hater • *The Mugger* • *The Pusher* (1956) *The Con Man* • *Killer's Choice* (1957) *Killer's Payoff* • *Killer's Wedge* • *Lady Killer* (1958) *'Til Death* • *King's Ransom* (1959) *Give the Boys a Great Big Hand* • *The Heckler* • *See Them Die* (1960) *Lady, Lady, I Did It!* (1961) *The Empty Hours* • *Like Love* (1962) *Ten Plus One* (1963) *Ax* (1964) *He Who Hesitates* • *Doll* (1965) *Eighty Million Eyes* (1966) *Fuzz* (1968) *Shotgun* (1969) *Jigsaw* (1970) *Hail, Hail, the Gang's All Here* (1971) *Sadie When She Died* • *Let's Hear It for the Deaf Man* (1972) *Hail to the Chief* (1973) *Bread* (1974) *Blood Relatives* (1975) *So Long As You Both Shall Live* (1976) *Long Time No See* (1977) *Calypso* (1979) *Ghosts* (1980) *Heat* (1981) *Ice* (1983) *Lightning* (1984) *Eight Black Horses* (1985) *Poison* • *Tricks* (1987) *Lullaby* (1989) *Vespers* (1990) *Widows* (1991) *Kiss* (1992) *Mischief* (1993) *And All Through the House* (1994) *Romance* (1995) *Nocturne* (1997) *The Big Bad City* (1999) *The Last Dance* (2000) *Money, Money, Money* (2001) *Fat Ollie's Book* (2003) *The Frumious Bandersnatch* • *Hark!* (2004)

The Matthew Hope Novels

Goldilocks (1978) *Rumpelstiltskin* (1981) *Beauty and the Beast* (1982) *Jack and the Beanstalk* (1984) *Snow White and Rose Red* (1985) *Cinderella* (1986) *Puss in Boots* (1987) *The House That Jack Built* (1988) *Three Blind Mice* (1990) *Mary, Mary* (1993) *There Was a Little Girl* (1994) *Gladly the Cross-Eyed Bear* (1996) *The Last Best Hope* (1998)

Other Novels

The Sentries (1965) *Where There's Smoke* • *Doors* (1975) *Guns* (1976) *Another Part of the City* (1986) *Downtown* (1991) *Driving Lessons* (2000) *Candyland* (2001) *Alice in Jeopardy* (2005)

Collections

Learning to Kill (2006)

Fiddlers

A Novel of
the 87th Precinct

Ed McBain

A Harvest Book
An Otto Penzler Book
Harcourt, Inc.
Orlando Austin New York
San Diego Toronto London

www.HarcourtBooks.com

The Library of Congress has cataloged the hardcover edition as follows:
McBain, Ed, 1926–
Fiddlers: a novel of the 87th Precinct/Ed McBain.—1st ed.
p. cm.
"An Otto Penzler Book."
1. Carella, Steve (Fictitious character)—Fiction. 2. 87th Precinct (Imaginary place)—Fiction. 3. Police—United States—Fiction. 4. Shooters of firearms—Fiction. 5. Serial murders—Fiction. I. Title.
PS3515.U585F525 2005
813'.54—dc22 2005004255
ISBN-13: 978-0-15-101216-9 ISBN-10: 0-15-101216-4
ISBN-13: 978-0-15-603278-0 (pbk.) ISBN-10: 0-15-603278-3 (pbk.)

Text set in Adobe Caslon
Designed by Kaelin Chappell Broaddus

Printed in the United States of America

First Harvest edition 2006
A C E G I K J H F D B

This is for my wife,

DRAGICA—

Here, now, forever

The city in these pages is imaginary.
The people, the places are all fictitious.
Only the police routine is based on
established investigatory technique.

Fiddlers

1.

The manager of Ninotchka was a wiseguy named Dominick La Paglia. Not a made man, but mob-connected, with a string of arrests dating back to when he was seventeen. Served time on two separate occasions, once for assault with intent, the other for dealing drugs. He insisted the club was clean, you couldn't even buy an inhaler in the place.

"We get an older crowd here," La Paglia said. "Ninotchka is all about candlelight and soft music. A balalaika band, three violinists wandering from table to table during intermission, the old folks holding hands when they're not on the floor dancing. Never any trouble here, go ask your buddies up Narcotics."

"Tell us about Max Sobolov," Carella said.

This was now eleven P.M. on Wednesday night, the sixteenth day of June. The three men were standing in the alleyway where the violinist had been shot twice in the face.

"What do you want to know?" La Paglia asked.

"How long was he working here?"

"Long time. Two years?"

"You hired a blind violinist, right?"

"Why not?"

"To wander from table to table, right?"

"Place is dark, anyway, what difference would it make to a blind man?" La Paglia said. "He played violin good. Got blinded in the Vietnam War, you know. Man's a war hero, somebody aces him in an alleyway."

"How about the other musicians working here? Any friction between Sobolov and them?" Meyer asked.

"No, he was blind," La Paglia said. "Everybody's very nice to blind people."

Except when they shoot them twice in the face, Carella thought.

"Or anybody else in the club? Any of the bartenders, waitresses, whoever?"

"Cloakroom girl?"

"Bouncer? Whoever?"

"No, he got along with everybody."

"So tell us what happened here tonight," Carella said.

"Were you here when he got shot?"

"I was here."

"Give us the sequence," Meyer said, and took out his notebook.

The way La Paglia tells it, the club closes at two in the morning every night of the week. The band plays its last set at one thirty, the violinists take their final stroll, angling for tips, at a quarter to. Bartenders have already served their last-call drinks, waitresses are already handing out the checks . . .

"You know the Irving Berlin line?" La Paglia asked. "'Before the fiddlers have fled'? One of the greatest lyrics ever written. That's what closing time is like. But this must've been around ten, ten thirty when Max went out for a smoke. We don't allow smoking in the club, half the geezers have emphysema, anyway. I was at the bar, talking to an old couple who are regulars, they never take a table, they always sit at the bar. It was a slow night, Wednesdays are always slow, they were talking about moving down to Florida. They were telling me all about Sarasota when I heard the shots."

"You recognized them as shots?"

La Paglia raised his eyebrows.

Come on, his look said. You think I don't know shots when I hear them?

"No," he said sarcastically. "I thought they were backfires, right?"

"What'd you do?"

"I ran out in the alley. He was already dead. Laying on his back, blood all over his face. White cane on the ground near his right hand."

"See anybody?"

"Sure, the killer hung around to be identified."

Meyer was thinking sarcasm didn't play too well on a mobster.

The Sobolov family was sitting shiva.

Meyer had been here, done this, but today was the first time Carella had ever been to a Jewish wake. He simply followed suit. When he saw Meyer taking off his shoes outside the open door to the apartment, he took off his shoes as well.

"The doors are left open so visitors can come in without distracting the mourners," Meyer told him. "No knocking or ringing of bells."

He was washing his hands in a small basin of water resting on a chair to the right of the door. Carella followed suit.

"I'm not a religious person," Meyer said. "I don't know why we wash our hands before going in."

This was all so very new to Carella. There were perhaps two dozen people in the Sobolov living room. Five of them were sitting on low benches. Meyer later explained that these were supplied by the funeral home. All of the mirrors in the house were covered with cloth, and a large candle was burning in one corner of the room.

In accordance with Jewish custom, Sobolov had been buried at once, and the family had begun sitting shiva as soon as they got home from the funeral. This was now Friday morning, the eighteenth day of June. The men in the family had not shaved. The women wore no makeup. There was a deep sense of loss in this house. Carella had been to Irish wakes, where the women keened, but where there was also laughter and much drinking. He had been to Italian wakes, where the women shrieked and tore at their clothing. The prevailing mood here was silent grief.

The apartment belonged to Max's younger brother and his wife. The brother's name was Sidney. The wife was Susan.

Both of Max's parents were dead, but there was an elderly uncle present, and also several cousins.

The uncle spoke with a heavy accent, Russian or Middle European, it was difficult to tell which. He told the detectives stories about when Max was still a little boy. How his parents had purchased for him a toy violin that Max took to at once . . .

"You should have seen him, a regular Yehudi Menuhin!"

The brother Sidney told them that his parents had immediately started Max taking lessons . . .

"On a *real* violin, never mind a toy," the uncle said.

. . . and within months he was playing complicated violin pieces . . .

"His teacher was astonished!"

"He had such an aptitude," one of the cousins said.

"A natural," Sidney agreed. "He was so sensitive, so feeling."

"The kindest person."

"Such a sweet little boy."

"When he played, your heart could melt."

"All his goodness came out in his playing."

"What a player!" the uncle said.

Sidney told them that no one was surprised when his brother was accepted at the Kleber School, or when Kusmin put him in his private class. "Alexei Kusmin," he explained. "The head of violin studies there."

"Max had a wonderful career ahead of him."

"But then, of course . . ." one of the cousins said.

"He got drafted."

"The war," his uncle said, and clucked his tongue.

"Vietnam."

"Twenty-fifth Infantry Division."

"Second Brigade."

"D Company."

"*B* Company, it was."

"No, Sidney, it was D."

"I used to write to him, it was B."

"All right, already. Whatever it was, he came back blind."

"Dreadful," Susan said, and shook her head.

"It began at the hospital," his uncle said. "The drug use."

"Before then," his brother said. "It started over there. In Vietnam."

"But mostly, it was the hospital."

"Medicinal," his brother said, nodding.

"The VA hospital."

This was the first the detectives were hearing about drug use.

They listened.

"And also, you know, musicians," one of the cousins said. "It's prevalent."

"But mostly the pain," the uncle said.

"Understandable," another cousin said.

"Besides, everybody smokes a little grass every now and then," a third cousin said.

"It should only be just a little grass," the uncle said, and wagged his head sympathetically.

"And yet," his brother said, "right to the day he died, he was the sweetest, most loving person on earth."

"A wonderful human being."

"A mensch," the uncle agreed.

Only one of the girls was really beautiful, but the other one was cute, too. He hadn't expected either of them to be prizes. You call an escort service, they're not about to send you a couple of movie stars.

The woman on the phone yesterday had said, "You know what this is gonna cost you, man?"

She sounded black.

"Price is no object," he'd said.

"Just so you know, it's a thousand for each girl for the night. Comes to two K, plus a tip is customary."

"No problem," he'd said.

"Usually twenty percent."

He thought this was high, but he said nothing.

"Which'll come to twenty-four hundred total. You could make it an even twenty-five, you were feeling generous."

"Credit card okay?" he'd asked.

"American Express, Visa, or MasterCard," she'd said. "What time did you want them?"

"Seven sharp," he'd said. "Can you make it a blonde and a redhead?"

"How about a nice Chinese girl?"

"No, not tonight."

"Or a luscious sistuh?"

He wondered if she had herself in mind.

"Just a blonde and a redhead. In their twenties, please."

"Le'me find you suppin nice," she'd said.

The blonde was the real beauty. She told him her name was Trish. He didn't think this was her real name. The redhead was the cute one. She said her name was Reggie, short for Regina, which he had to believe because who on earth would chose Regina as a phony name? He guessed Trish was in her mid-twenties. Reggie said she was nineteen. He believed that, too.

"So what are we planning to do here tonight?" Trish asked.

She was the bubbly one. Wearing a short little black cocktail dress, high-heeled black sandals. Reggie was wearing green, to match her green eyes. Serious look on her Irish phizz, she should have been wearing glasses. Better legs than Trish, cute little cupcake breasts as opposed to the melons Trish was bouncing around. Neither of them was wearing a bra. They both wandered the hotel suite like it was the Taj Mahal.

"Lookee here, two bedrooms!" Trish said. "We can try both of them!"

Before morning, they'd used both beds, and the big Jacuzzi tub in the marbled bathroom. It hadn't worked anywhere.

"Why don't we try it again tonight?" Trish suggested now.

"I have other plans," he told her.

"Then how about tomorrow night?" she said.

"Maybe," he said.

"Well, think about it," she said, and gave his limp cock a playful little tug, and then went off to shower. Reggie was drinking coffee at the dining room table, wearing just her panties, tufts of wild red hair curling around the leg holes. Freckles on her bare little breasts. Nipples puckered.

"We could do this alone sometime, you know," she said.

He looked at her.

"Just you and me. Sometimes it works better alone."

He kept looking at her.

"Sometimes two girls are intimidating. Alone, we could do things we didn't try last night."

"Like what?"

"Oh, I don't know. We'll experiment."

"We will, huh?"

"If you want to," she said. "Give it another try, you know?" She lifted her coffee cup, drank, put it down on the table again. "And you wouldn't have to go through the service," she said.

Down the hall, he could hear the shower going.

"You could call me direct," she said, "forget Sophisticates," and shoved back her chair and walked to the counter, and began writing on the hotel pad under the wall phone. Leaning over the counter, writing. White panties tight across her firm little ass. Nineteen years old. She tore the top sheet of paper from the pad, turned to him and grinned. Little Bugs Bunny grin. Freckles spattered on her cheeks and nose. Strutted back to the table barefooted. Plunked down the sheet of paper like a warrant.

"Call me," she said.

He picked up her number, looked at it.

"Whenever," she said, serious now, the grin gone.

"Well, not tonight," he said.

Tonight he would have to kill Alicia Hendricks.

He was worried that he wouldn't have the strength to see him through all this. Not the mental conviction, no, not that—he *knew* he was doing the right thing, was convinced of that the moment he decided on what had to be done *now,* if ever, so that he could at last come to terms with what he bitterly labeled his so-called life. But would he have the actual *physical* strength he would need to carry him through to the end?

The corrections had to be made, however painful.

Yes. All the decisions not his own, all the paths traveled against his will, all the journeys to places he had not chosen for himself, these had to be adjusted. *Now.* They had to learn he was cognizant of the sins committed, they had to be made to realize. Even blind Sobolov, who could not see who was about to fire two shots into his face, had recognized in that last moment that this was redemption, had whispered a name on the sullen night air—"Charlie?"—just before the thunder roared and the blood spurted.

The problem now was staying strong.

Not allowing the pain to divert him.

Then he would get through this.

Louis Hawkins was asleep when Carella and Meyer knocked on his door at noon that Friday.

He told them at once that he'd worked till two A.M. last night, and didn't get home till three, and he appreciated his sleep and didn't much care for the police knocking on his door at the crack of dawn. Carella apologized for both cops, explained the urgency of constructing a timetable before a case got cold, and then politely asked if Hawkins could spare them a few moments of his time. Reluctantly, he let them into the apartment.

All over the walls, there were photographs of a balding, gray-haired man playing a violin.

"Stephane Grappelli," Hawkins explained. "You want coffee? What the hell, I'm awake now."

Barefooted and in his bathrobe, he stood at the kitchen counter, measuring out coffee by the spoonful.

"Greatest jazz violinist who ever lived," he said. "Died in Paris seven years ago. Still playing when he was eighty-nine. You know what he said when he was eighty-five? A reporter asked him if he was considering retirement. Grappelli said, 'Retirement! There isn't a word that's more painful to my ears. Music keeps me going. It has given me everything. It's my fountain of youth.' I feel the same way. I'm almost fifty, lots of people start considering a condo in Florida at that age. Hell, I could get a job down there easy, same as the one I have here at Ninotchka, playing gypsy music for old farts. But you know something? I moonlight at jazz clubs. Sit in with some of the best musicians in this city. That's what keeps me going. You ever hear of Django Reinhardt? The great jazz guitarist? You never heard of him?"

"I heard of him," Carella said.

"Grappelli used to play with him. Can you imagine *that* sound? They took the world by storm! The stuff they did with the quintet? At the Hot Club in Paris? Nothing like it, man, nothing on earth. He's my hero. If I could ever play like him . . ." Hawkins let the sentence trail. "I hope you like it strong," he said, and set the coffeepot on the stove to perk. "So this is about Max, huh?"

"It's about Max," Meyer said.

"I figured. You know what Grappelli once said? He said, 'I play best when I'm happy or sad.' I think Max played best when he was sad. In fact, I don't think I ever saw him happy."

"Sad about what?" Carella asked.

"His lost sight? His lost youth? All his lost opportunities? When he played gypsy music, he made you want to weep. The codgers tipped him lavishly, believe me."

"What lost opportunities?" Meyer asked.

"He had a great career ahead of him as a classical musician. Before he got drafted, he was studying with Alexei Kusmin at the Kleber School of Music here. Max was one of the more promising young violinists around. Then . . . Vietnam."

"Any idea why anyone would want him dead?"

"Senseless," Hawkins said, and shook his head. "You want some orange juice?" Without waiting for an answer, he went to the refrigerator, took out a bottle. "This is fresh-squeezed," he said, pouring. "I get it at the organic market, it's not from concentrate. I mean, who would want to kill a blind man? Why? Grappelli also said he played best when he was young and in love. I don't think Max was ever in love. In fact, I don't think he was ever young. The army grabbed him for Vietnam, and that was the end of his youth, the end of everything. He came back blind. Tell that to all these fuckin macho presidents who send young kids off to fight their stupid fuckin wars."

"What makes you say he'd never been in love?" Carella asked.

"Do *you* see a woman in his life? I'm sorry, but I don't see one. A wife? A girlfriend? Do you see one? I see a guy who was fifty, sixty years old, wandering around in the dark with a violin tucked under his chin, playing music could break your heart. That's what I see. This is done. How do you take it?"

They sat at the kitchen table, drinking coffee.

Hawkins was silent for what seemed a long time. Then he said, "Grappelli once said, 'I forget everything when I play. I split into two people and the other plays.' I had the feeling Max did the same thing. I think when he played, he forgot whatever it was that troubled him."

"And what was that?" Meyer asked.

"Well, we'll never know, now will we?"

"Did he ever specifically mention anything that was bothering him?"

"Never. Not to me. Maybe to some of the other musicians. But I have to tell you, Max kept mostly to himself. It was as if his blindness locked him away in darkness. You ask me, the only time he expressed himself was when he was playing. The rest of the time . . ." Hawkins shook his head. "Silence."

On the way down to the street, Carella said, "The rest is silence."

Meyer looked at him.

"Hamlet," Carella said. "I played Claudius in a college production."

"I didn't know that."

"Yeah. I could've been famous."

"I'll bet."

They came out into the street, began walking toward where they'd parked the car.

"How about you?" Carella asked.

"I could've been Picasso."

"Yeah?"

"When I was a kid, I wanted to be an artist," Meyer said, and shrugged.

"Ever regret becoming a cop?"

"A cop? No. Hey, no. You?"

"No," Carella said. "No."

They walked toward the car in silence, thinking about paths not taken, dreams unborn.

"Well, let's check out this other musician," Carella said.

"I play at Ninotchka only when I'm between pit gigs," Sy Handelman told them.

They figured a "pit gig" was a job that was the bottom of the barrel. The pits.

"The orchestra pit," Handelman explained. "For musicals downtown, on the Stem."

He was twenty years old or so. Wore his hair long, like an anachronistic hippie. They could imagine him playing violin outside a theater downtown, collecting tips in a plate on the sidewalk. A busker. They could also imagine him in a long-sleeved, white-silk, ruffled shirt, playing violin for the senior citizens at Ninotchka. They had a little more trouble visualizing him in the orchestra pit at a hit musical; on their salaries they rarely got to see hundred-dollar-ticket shows.

"I like pit work," Handelman said. "All those good-looking gypsies."

They got confused again.

Was he now talking about his work at Ninotchka?

"The chorus girls," he explained. "We call them gypsies. You sit in the orchestra pit, you can see up their dresses clear to Manderlay."

"Must be an interesting line of work," Meyer said.

"Can make you blind, you're not careful," Handelman said, and grinned.

Which led them to why they were here.

"Max Sobolov?" Handelman said. "A sad old Jew."

"He was only fifty-eight," Meyer said.

"There are sad old men who are only forty," Handelman observed philosophically.

"Ever tell you why he was so sad?" Carella asked.

"I got the feeling it was guilt. We Jews always feel guilty, anyway, am I right?" he said to Meyer. "But with Max, it was really oppressive. What I'm saying is nobody acts the way Max did unless he did something terrible he was sorry for. Never smiled. Hardly even said hello when he came to work. Just got into costume . . . we wear these red-silk ruffled shirts . . ."

Okay, so they'd figured white.

". . . and tight black pants, give the old ladies a thrill, you know. Then he went out to do his thing. Which was to play this dark, brooding, gypsy music. Which he did superbly, I must say."

"We understand he was trained as a classical musician."

"I didn't know that, but I'm not surprised. Where, would you know?"

"Kleber."

"The best. I'm not surprised."

"This terrible thing he did, whatever it was . . ."

"Well, I'm just guessing."

"Did he ever mention what it might have been, specifically?"

"No. He never told me any of this, you understand, he never said, 'Gee, I'm so guilty and sad because I threw my teenage sweetheart off the roof,' never anything like that. But there was this . . . this abiding sense of guilt about him. Guilt and grief. Yes. Grief. As if he was so very sorry."

"For what?" Carella asked.

"Maybe for himself," Handelman said.

First time Kling ever called her was from a phone booth in the rain. Less a booth, really, than one of these little plastic shells, rain pouring down around him. He was calling from a similar enclosure today, the heat rising from the pavement in shimmering waves he could actually see, talk about palpable.

He hadn't spoken to her in six days, but who was counting? You go from sharing apartments, his and hers, alternately, to simply not speaking, that was a very serious contrast. He was calling her at her office, he hoped he wouldn't get the usual medical menu, hoped he wouldn't get a nurse asking him where he itched or hurt. Sharyn Cooke was the police department's Deputy Chief Surgeon. Bert Kling was a Detective/Third Grade. Big enough difference right there. Never mind the fact that she was black and he was white. Blond, no less.

"Dr. Cooke's office," a female voice said.

He was calling her uptown, in Diamondback, where she had her private practice. Her police office was in Rankin

Plaza, across the river. They knew him at both places. Or at least *used* to know him. He hoped she hadn't given orders otherwise.

"Hi," he said, "it's Bert. May I speak to her, please?"

"Just a moment, please."

He almost said, "Jenny, is that you?" Knew all the nurses. But she was gone. He waited. And waited. Heat rose from the sidewalk and the street.

"Hello?"

"Sharyn?" he said.

"Yes, Bert."

"How are you?"

"Fine, thanks."

"Shar . . ."

Silence.

"I'd like to see you."

More silence.

"Shar, we have to talk."

"I can't talk yet," she said.

"Shar . . ."

"I'm still too hurt."

Heat rising.

"You don't know how much you hurt me," she said.

Fire truck going by somewhere on the street. Siren blaring.

"Please don't call me for a while," she said.

There was a click on the line.

For a while, he thought.

He guessed that was a hopeful sign.

Alicia was certain someone was following her. She'd confided this to her boss, who told her she was nuts. "Who'd want to follow you?" he'd said, which she considered a bit of an insult. Like *what*? She wasn't good-looking enough to be followed?

Alicia was fifty-five years old, a tall Beauty Plus blonde (what they called Honey Melt, actually) with excellent legs and fine breasts, a woman who'd provoked many a construction-worker whistle on the streets of this fair city—so what had Jamie meant by his remark? Besides, she *was* being followed, she was certain of that. In fact, she checked the street this way and that the minute she stepped out onto the sidewalk that Friday evening.

Beauty Plus was located in a twenty-seven-story building on Twombley Street midtown. The Lustre Nails Care Division was located in a string of eight offices on the seventeenth floor of the building. Fanning out from these offices every weekday were the twenty-two sales reps Beauty Plus hoped would vigorously sell its nail-care products to the four-thousand-plus manicure salons all over the city. Alicia had written out her day's report by a quarter to five, had mentioned to Jamie Dewes that she hoped she wouldn't be followed again tonight (hence his snide remark) and was stepping out onto the sidewalk at a few minutes past five.

The June heat hit her like a closed fist.

She looked up and down the street again. No sign of whoever it was she felt sure was following her. She stepped out in a long-legged stride, heading for the subway kiosk on the next corner.

Detective/First Grade Oliver Wendell Weeks had lost ten pounds. This caused him to look merely like a hippopotamus. Patricia Gomez thought he was making real progress.

"This is truly remarkable, Oll," she told him. "Ten pounds in two weeks, do you know how wonderful that is?"

Ollie did not think it was so wonderful.

Ollie felt hungry all the time.

Patricia was still in uniform. She told Ollie she'd signed out late because her sergeant had something brilliant to say about the way the team had handled a joint operation with Street Crime. Seemed a confidential informant wasn't where he was supposed to be when the bust went down, some such bullshit. Her sergeant was always complaining about something or other, the old hairbag. Ollie told her he'd have a word with the man, ah yes, get him off her case. Patricia told him to never mind. They were strolling up Culver Av, in the Eight-Eight territory they called home during their working day. If she wasn't in uniform, he'd have been holding her hand.

"Are you nervous about tonight?" she asked.

"No," he said. "Why should I be nervous?"

Actually, he was nervous.

"You don't have to be," she said, and took his hand, uniform or not.

On the way to Calm's Point, Alicia kept eyeing the subway crowd. The man who'd been following her was bald, she was sure of that. More of a Patrick Stewart bald than a Bruce Willis bald. Tall slender guy with a slick bald pate, had to be in his mid-to-late fifties.

He scared hell out of her.

She'd spotted him on two separate occasions now, just quick glimpses, each time ducking out of sight when she'd turned to look.

There was only one bald guy in the subway car, and he had to be in his seventies, sitting there reading a Spanish-language newspaper.

Ollie guessed he expected everybody to be speaking Spanish. Her mother's name was Catalina, and her two sisters were Isabella and Enriquetta. Her brother—who played piano—was named Alonso. First thing the brother said was, "Hey, dude, I hear you play piano, too."

"Well, a little," Ollie said modestly.

"He learned 'Spanish Eyes' for me," Patricia said, beaming.

"Get *out*!" her sister said.

"I mean it, he'll play it for us later."

"Well," Ollie said modestly.

"Come," Patricia's mother said, "have some *bacalaítos*."

Ollie almost said he was on a diet, but Patricia gave him an okay nod.

The owner of the Korean grocery store around the corner from her apartment greeted Alicia warmly when she stopped in to pick up some things for dinner. He told her he had some nice fresh blueberries today, three-ninety-nine a basket. She bought half a pound of shiitake mushrooms, a dozen eggs, a container of low-fat milk, and two baskets of the berries.

It was while she was making herself an omelet that she heard the bedroom window sliding open.

"Oh, Spanish eyes . . ."

This was the Al Martino version of the song, not the one the Backstreet Boys did years later. Ollie had been studying it for weeks now. His piano teacher insisted he had it down pat, but this was the first time he'd ever performed it in public, in front of Patricia's whole family, no less.

They were all gathered around the upright piano in the Gomez living room. A framed picture of Jesus was on the piano top. The picture made Ollie nervous, staring at him that way. What made him even more nervous was Patricia's father. Ollie got the feeling her father didn't like him too much. Probably thought Ollie was going to violate his virgin daughter, though Ollie guessed she wasn't one at all.

Patricia and her mother knew the words by heart. It was Patricia's mother, in fact, who'd taught her the song. Her sister Isabella seemed to be hearing it for the first time. She seemed to like it, kept swaying back and forth to it. When they'd met tonight, Ollie told her his sister's name was Isabel, too, and she'd said, "Get out!" She looked a little like Patricia, but Patricia was prettier. Nobody in the family was as good-looking as Patricia. In fact, nobody in this entire city was as good-looking as Patricia.

Tito Gomez, the father, kept scowling at Ollie.

The brother was doing a good imitation of his father, too.

Patricia and her mother kept singing along.

Isabella kept swaying to the music.

In the kitchen, *asopao de pollo* was cooking.

At first, Alicia thought she was hearing things. She'd turned on the air conditioner and closed all the windows the minute she'd come into the apartment, but now she heard what sounded like a window going up in the bedroom. There were two windows in the bedroom, one of them opening on the fire escape, the other with an air-conditioning unit in it. She did not want to believe that someone had just opened the fire escape window, but . . .

"Hello?" she called.

From outside, she heard the sudden rush of traffic below. Would she be hearing traffic if the window wasn't . . . ?

"Hello?" she said again.

"Hello, Alicia," a voice called.

A man's voice.

She froze to the spot.

She'd sliced the mushrooms with a big carving knife, and she lifted that from the counter now, and was backing away toward the entrance door to the apartment when he came out of the bedroom. There was a large gun in his right hand. There was some kind of thing fastened to the barrel. An instant before he spoke, she recognized it as a silencer.

"Remember me?" he said. "Chuck?"

And shot her twice in the face.

2.

The two detectives met for lunch in a diner on Albermarle, two hours after Carella received the telephone call. He figured he knew what Kramer wanted. He wasn't wrong.

"The thing is," Kramer was telling him, "we don't catch many homicides up the Nine-Eight. This is more up your alley, you know what I mean."

Low crime rate in the Nine-Eight, was what Kramer was saying. As compared to the soaring statistics uptown in the asshole of creation, was what Kramer was saying. What's another homicide more or less to you guys, Kramer was saying. Carella was inclined to tell him, Thanks, pal, but our platter is full right now. If only it weren't for the First Man Up rule.

Kramer wouldn't have called if the Ballistics match hadn't come through so fast. You get a blind man shot dead outside a nightclub Wednesday night, and then Friday night, at the other end of the city, you get a woman killed cooking an omelet in her own apartment, there's no connection, right? Unless Ballistics calls early Monday morning to tell you the same nine-millimeter Glock was used in both shootings. That can capture a person's attention, all right. It had certainly caught Kramer's, who was now munching on a ham and egg sandwich while trying not to be too aggressive about the department's time-honored First Man Up rule. Hence his song and dance about the Nine-Eight's inexperience with matters homicidal.

"So what do you say?" he asked Carella. "I'll turn over our paper to you, the Eight-Seven can pick it up from there. This should be a snap for you guys, you already got a gun match."

A snap, Carella thought, and wondered how many nines were loose in the city.

"I'd have to check with the loot," he said, "see if he thinks we can take on another homicide just now."

"Oh, sure," Kramer said, and then casually added, "but he's familiar with FMU, of course." And further added, "Which is the case here. You caught your blind guy two days before we caught the omelet lady. So what do you say?" Kramer asked again.

He knew he had Carella dead to rights on FMU. He was just being polite.

Carella hoped he'd at least pay for the lunch.

"Way I understand this," Parker said, "is we're now the garbage can of the Detective Division, is that it?"

There were only five men in the lieutenant's office and Parker had the floor. He was dressed this Monday afternoon the way he usually dressed for work: like a bum. Unshaven. Blue jeans and a T-shirt. Short-sleeved Hawaiian print shirt over that, but only to hide the automatic holstered at his right hip.

"I wouldn't put it exactly that way," Carella said.

"No? Then what does it mean when any murder done with a Glock gets dumped on us?"

"Not *every* Glock. Just the ones that match the blind-man kill."

"Which we caught," Lieutenant Byrnes explained again. Bullet-headed, gray-haired, square-jawed, he looked like an older Dick Tracy sitting behind his corner-office desk. "Which means First Man Up prevails," he explained further.

"Like I said," Parker continued, undeterred. "We're the DD's garbage can."

"How many have there been so far?" Genero asked. Curly-haired, brown-eyed, the youngest man on the squad, he always sounded tentative. Or maybe just stupid.

"Just two, counting the omelet lady."

"That ain't so many," Genero said. "Can you run them by us?" he said, trying to sound executive.

"The blind guy is the one we caught," Meyer said. "Ten thirty last Wednesday night."

Bald and burly, shirtsleeves rolled up and shirt collar open because the squadroom's air conditioner wasn't working again on one of the hottest days this June, he hunched over Carella's desk, consulting the DD report.

"That would've been?"

"June sixteenth."

"Fifty-eight years old. Two in the head," Meyer said.

"From a Glock?"

"A Glock. Apparently, nothing was stolen from him. His wallet still contained a check for three hundred dollars, and a hundred and change in cash, presumably tip money."

"And the next one?"

Carella walked over from the watercooler. He moved like an athlete, though he wasn't one, his skills limited to stickball when he was a kid growing up in Riverhead. He picked up the Nine-Eight's report, and studied it again, together with the other detectives this time. Standing side by side, reading the report, the men could have been accountants looking over a client's weekly payroll report—if only it weren't for the shoulder holsters.

And the nine-millimeter Glocks in them.

Just like the one that killed the omelet lady and the blind guy.

"Friday night," Carella said. "Calm's Point. The Nine-Eight phoned this morning, right after they got a Ballistics match."

"Sure, the word's out," Parker said. "Dump it on the Eight-Seven."

"Perp climbed in the window and shot her while she was cooking an omelet," Meyer said.

"What kind of omelet was it?" Genero asked.

Parker looked at him.

"I'm curious."

"Who was the vic?" Parker asked.

"Woman named Alicia Hendricks. Fifty-five years old."

"Point is," Byrnes said, "Steve and Meyer can't handle it alone. We're looking at overtime here. Two homicides in as many . . ."

"Like I said, we're the garbage can here," Parker said.

"How do you want us to divvy this, Loot?" Carella asked.

"I thought Andy and Richard could get on the latest one . . ."

"Who caught it again?" Genero asked.

"The Nine-Eight. Detective up there named Kramer."

"Like in *Seinfeld*?"

"There's other Kramers in this world, Richard."

"Like I didn't know, Andy."

"You and Meyer stick with the violin player. And head up the team."

"We better hope there ain't another one," Parker said.

"Another violin player?" Genero asked.

"Another *anybody*," Parker said.

This was truly a pain in the ass.

Calm's Point could have been a foreign nation. Took them forty minutes downtown from the Eight-Seven and then over the bridge to the Nine-Eight, where the most recent Glock murder had occurred. Was what they were already calling them: The Glock Murders. In the dead woman's apartment now, the inheriting detectives felt like they'd just crossed the Euphrates.

The body had been removed long ago, but its chalked

outline was still on the kitchen floor. Frying pan on the stove, cold mushrooms and eggs in it, lady'd been cooking an omelet. Big carving knife on the floor, where she'd dropped it when the killer aced her. Fire escape window open wide, they assumed this had been the point of entry.

What troubled them was that this time he—or she—had been invasive. The blind violinist had been shot on the street. This time, the killer had entered the vic's living space, which meant this wasn't just a random killing, this was a chosen target. Which could or could not mean that the previous vic had been deliberately selected as well. In which case, the killer had so far picked targets in disparate parts of the city. The blind guy all the way uptown in the Eight-Seven's turf, and now the omelet lady, here in her own apartment in Calm's Point.

No apparent theft this time, either. Lady's jewelry still in her top dresser drawer, money in her handbag. Credit cards ID'd her as one Alicia Hendricks. Neighbors told them she worked for some cosmetics company in "The City"—which meant back across the river and into the trees again. One of the neighbors thought the name of the firm was Beauty Blush. But a laminated card in her wallet identified her as a sales rep for a firm called Beauty *Plus,* at 165 Twombley, in midtown Isola, and a phone call confirmed that she was indeed an employee of the company.

The salesman was telling him that the sticker price on the car was $74,330 . . .

"Standard features include the four-point-two-liter V-8, two-hundred and ninety-four horsepower engine . . ."

Baldy kept circling the car like some kind of hawk about to pounce on a rabbit.

"... six-speed automatic transmission with overdrive, four-wheel antilock brakes ..."

Guy didn't look like he could afford seventy-four *bucks,* no less seventy-four *grand* ...

"... side-seat-mounted air bags, driver and passenger side air-bag head extension ..."

"What colors does it come in?" Baldy asked.

"I have the chart right here," the salesman said. "Your exteriors come in the Topaz, the Ebony, the Midnight, the Radiance, the Seafrost ..."

Guy kept circling the car, running the palm of his hand over the fenders, the hood, the sleek sides ...

"For the interiors, you have a choice of the Cashmere, the Dove, the Ivory ..."

"When can I take delivery?"

"Depends on whether you plan to buy or lease ..."

"Lease," Baldy said.

"... and whether we can find the vehicle in the colors you ..."

"Find it," he said.

The sales manager of Beauty Plus's Lustre Nails Care Division was a man named Jamie Dewes. He was surprised to find two detectives from uptown on his doorstep at four P.M. that twenty-first day of June, because he'd already been visited by detectives from Calm's Point last week.

"Terrible thing," he told Parker and Genero. "Why would anyone want to kill Alicia?"

But in the very next breath, he told the detectives that Alicia thought someone was following her. Veronica Alston, his assistant, confirmed this.

"Some creepy bald-headed guy," she said.

"When did she tell you this?" Genero asked.

"Last week sometime?" Jamie said.

"No, before then," Veronica said. "Around the beginning of the month."

"What a month," Jamie said. "Hottest damn June I can remember."

"Said someone was following her?" Parker said.

"Said she'd spotted this guy following her, yes."

"Where, did she say?"

"Just following her."

"Here? This neighborhood? Or where she lived?"

"She didn't say."

"How many times did she spot him?"

"Once or twice."

"Did she confront him?"

"No. Well, I don't think so."

"Did she report any of this to the police?"

"No. Ronnie? She didn't call the police, did she?"

"No," Veronica said.

"Just mentioned it to each of you."

"Yes."

"Either of you notice any bald guys lurking around outside?" Parker asked.

They both shook their heads.

"Know anything about anyone she might've been seeing?" he asked. "Any boyfriends?"

"She recently broke up with this stockbroker guy," Veronica said.

"Would you know his name?"

"No. Harold something."

"When was this?"

"Breaking up? Around Easter time."

"Been dating anyone since?"

Jamie shrugged.

So did Veronica.

"This Harold something? He wouldn't be bald, would he?"

"Don't know what he looks like," Veronica said, and shrugged again.

"Would anyone else in the office know his last name?"

One of the other sales reps did.

Harold Saperstein was a man in his early fifties, they guessed. Wearing eyeglasses and a business suit. He had thick curly black hair, they noticed.

He was just leaving his office when they caught up with him at five that Monday afternoon. They identified themselves, told him they were investigating the murder of Alicia Hendricks . . .

"Yeah, I figured you'd be around," he said.

. . . and asked if he would mind answering a few questions. They walked over to a pocket park near his office. The three men sat on a bench, Saperstein in the middle. A waterfall streamed down a tan brick wall behind them. It made the day seem cooler.

"So tell us how you happened to break up," Parker said.

"You know about that, huh?"

"Tell us, anyway," Genero said.

"It was *The Passion.*"

They thought he was talking about the heat of their love affair.

"The Mel Gibson movie," he explained. "I told Alicia it was anti-Semitic. She disagreed. I'm Jewish, we got into an argument."

"So whose idea was it to split up?"

"My mother's. I live with my mother. She said if we were going to fight already over a fecockteh movie, that was just the beginning."

"When was this?"

"Around Easter time. When the fever was at its pitch."

"When's the last time you saw her?"

"Passover. At my mother's."

"Ever talk to her since?"

"Yes."

"When?"

"Couple of weeks ago. She phoned to tell me some guy was following her."

"And?"

"She wanted to know what she should do. I told her to call the cops."

"Did she?"

"I have no idea. That's the last time we ever spoke."

He was silent for a while. Behind them, the water cascaded down the wall.

"I *hate* Mel Gibson," he said.

"This would've been a long time ago," Meyer said.

"Forty years or more."

"Around the time of the Vietnam War."

The woman they were talking to was Abigail Nelson, Director of Music Studies at the Kleber School of Music, Dance and Drama. She was perhaps forty years old, a trim-looking woman who wore her darkish brown hair in a feather cut. Blue pinstripe suit, like what you'd expect on a bank manager. Alert blue eyes behind oversized glasses. They were sitting at a long table in the school's clerical office. Filing cabinets lined the room. Late afternoon sunlight slanted through the windows. Down the hall, they could hear distant music from rehearsal rooms.

"The sixties sometime?" Abigail asked.

"Mid-sixties, probably. We have him in Vietnam during the late sixties."

"So this would've been before then."

"Yes."

"We wouldn't even have been in this building. In the sixties, we were still uptown, on Silvermine Drive, near Tenth."

"Close to our turf," Meyer said. "The precinct."

"Yes," Abigail said, not completely sure she'd understood. "He was a violin major, did you say?"

"Yes."

"Alexei Kusmin would have been heading Violin Studies."

"Yes, so we understand. Mr. Sobolov was one of his students."

"Kusmin was first desk at the philharmonic back then. But he also taught here. Your man would have played violin day in and day out for four years. Well, not just violin. He'd have taken piano as his second instrument, all students in the music department do, even today. And L and M, of course, which is Literature and Materials. He'd also have played in one of the orchestras. There were only two back then, the Concert and the Rep. We have four now. And he'd have taken courses in music history, and—since he was a string musician—he'd have been assigned to chamber music as well."

"He'd have been busy," Carella said.

"Oh yes. Our students are expected to be *serious* about music. Here at Kleber, it's music—or dance or drama, of course—all day long, every day of the week. Lessons, or practicing, or performing in this or that orchestra . . . it's a life, gentlemen. It's a full life."

The detectives nodded.

Carella was wondering if he ever really could have become a famous actor.

Meyer was thinking his uncle Isadore had once told him he made nice drawings.

As she led them across the room, Abigail explained that Max Sobolov's options after a four-year course of study here would have been numerous.

"We've got several major symphony orchestras in this city, you know," she said, "plus the two opera companies, and the three ballets. There are something like thirty, thirty-five violin chairs in any given orchestra—well, count them. Eighteen fiddles in the first section, another fifteen in the second. That's thirty-three chances for a job in any of the city's orchestras. Plus there's nothing to say he couldn't have applied to an orchestra in Chicago, or Cleveland, or wherever. A good violinist? And one of Kusmin's students? His chances would have been very good indeed."

She pulled open one of the file drawers.

"Let's hope his records haven't already been boxed and sent up to Archives," she said. "Soboloff, was it?"

"Sobolov," Carella said. "With an o-*v*."

"Ah. Yes," she said, and began riffling through the folders. When she found the one for SOBOLOV, MAX, she placed it on top of the filing cabinet, and opened it. "Yes," she said, "an excellent student. Brilliant future ahead of him." She paused, reading. "But you see, gentlemen, he never finished the course of study here. He left after only three years."

"The Army," Meyer said.

"Vietnam," Carella said.

"A pity," Abigail said.

"This would've been a long time ago, you understand," the woman in the clerical office was telling them.

Her name was Clara Whaitsley. Parker thought she was British at first, the name and all, and this was mildly exciting because he'd never been to bed with a British girl. But she had a broad Riverhead accent, and he'd been to bed with lots of Riverhead girls in his lifetime. So had Genero. Well, a few, anyway. All business, they merely listened to her.

"We're talking a girl in her teens," Clara said. "They enter high school in the tenth grade, you know, when they're fifteen, going on sixteen. According to our records, Alicia Hendricks came into Harding directly from Mercer Junior High, some forty years ago."

"Long time ago," Genero observed sagely.

"The usual progression is Pierce Elementary to Mercer Junior High to Harding High," Clara said. "We have her leaving Harding at sixteen."

"Any follow-up on that?"

"We wouldn't have anything on her after she left our school."

"Went into the workforce, looks like," Genero said.

"That's awfully young to be starting work."

"I started work when I was fourteen," Parker said.

He was tempted to add that he'd got laid for the first time when he was sixteen.

"You know," Clara said, "while I was looking through the files for you . . ."

Both detectives suddenly gave her their undivided attention.

". . . I came across the records for another Hendricks. I don't know if they're related or not, but he was here at about the same time, entered a year later."

"What've you got on him?" Parker asked.

Karl Hendricks was still serving the twelfth year of a fifteen-year rap. He'd been denied parole twice—the first time because he'd physically abused a prison guard, the second because he'd stabbed another inmate with a fork. He could not have been older than fifty-three or -four, but at six thirty that Monday evening, when he shuffled into the room where Genero and Parker were waiting for him, he looked like an old man.

"What is this?" he asked.

"Your sister was murdered," Parker told him subtly.

"Yeah?" Hendricks said.

He seemed only mildly interested.

"When's the last time you saw her?" Genero asked.

"Be a real miracle if I did it, now wun't it?" Hendricks said. "Sittin up here in stir."

"We're wondering who did," Parker said.

"Who cares?"

"We do."

"I don't."

"So when *did* you see her last?"

"She came to visit on my forty-fifth birthday. Brought me a cake with candles on it. No file inside it, more's the pity."

Sometimes, in prison, a man developed a sense of sarcastic humor. Sometimes the humor was funny.

"When was that, Karl?"

"Nine years ago. I'd just started serving this bum rap."

In prison, everyone was serving a bum rap. Nobody'd ever done the crime for which he'd been convicted. Nobody.

"Nine years ago," Genero said, and nodded, thinking it over.

It seemed unlikely that Alicia Hendricks would have mentioned anyone following her nine years ago. Nine years was a long time to be following someone. Nine years was what you might call a Dedicated Stalker. Genero asked, anyway.

"She mention anyone following her?"

Hendricks stared at him blankly.

"Some bald-headed guy following her?"

"No," Hendricks said, and shook his head unbelievingly.

"That why you came all the way up here? Cause some bald-headed guy was following her?"

"We came all the way up here because your sister got murdered," Parker said.

"I'm surprised somebody didn't kill her a long time ago," Hendricks said.

"Oh?"

"The friends she had. The company she kept."

"What kind of company?"

"Half of them should be in here doing time."

"Oh?"

"In fact, her first husband *did* do time, but not here."

"Husband? We've got her as single."

"Married twice," Hendricks said. "Both of them losers."

"Went back to using her maiden name, is that it?"

"Wouldn't you?"

"Tell us about these guys."

"The first one did time in Huntsville. One of the state prisons down there."

"That be in Texas?"

"Texas, yeah."

"For what?"

"Delivery and sale. Copped a plea, got off with two years and a five-grand fine."

"You ever meet this winner?"

"No. Alicia told me about him."

"So this had to be longer ago than nine years, right?"

"Huh?"

"If the last time she came to visit . . ."

"Oh. Yeah."

"So this first husband is bygone times, right?"

"Right."

"When did he do his time? Before or after Alicia knew him?"

"Before. He was out by the time they met."

"Living up here by then?"

"I guess. Otherwise how would she've met him?"

"That his only fall? The one in Texas?"

"Far as I know."

"And his name?"

"Al Dalton."

"For Albert?"

"Who the hell knows?"

"How about the second husband? Has he got a record, too?"

"No. What makes you think that?"

"Well, you said he was a loser."

"One thing has nothing to do with the other. I'm in jail, for example, but I'm not necessarily a loser."

Parker nodded sympathetically.

"But this second husband *was* a loser, you said."

"A loser, how?" Genero asked.

"Bad investments, like that. Also, he did dope."

"Ah," Parker said. "And Alicia?"

"She dabbled."

"Ah."

"What's his name? The second husband?"

"Ricky Montero. For Ricardo."

"A spic?" Parker said.

"Dominican."

"What kind of bad investments?"

"You name them."

"Is he still here in this country, or did he go back home?"

"Who knows? She divorced him, it's got to be ten, twelve years ago. I never liked him. He played trumpet."

"Is that why you didn't like him?"

"I got nothing against trumpet players. I'm just saying he played trumpet, is all."

"So that's the bad company she kept, right?" Genero said. "These two husbands. Al Dalton and Ricky Montero."

"I didn't say 'bad.' That's your word."

"You said half of her friends should be in here doing time."

"That don't make them bad."

"No, that makes them sweethearts."

"I'm doing time, and I ain't bad."

"No, all you did was stab somebody twelve years ago, and then stab somebody else, right here in jail, two years ago."

"That don't make you bad at all," Genero said.

"That makes you an angel," Parker said.

"You done breaking my balls? Cause I don't know who killed my sister, and I don't give a shit who did."

"Sit down," Parker said.

"Sit down," Genero said.

"Tell us who these *other* friends of hers were."

"From days of yore."

"These people who should be in here doing time."

"My sister started young," Hendricks said.

"Started *what* young? Dabbling in dope?"

"Started *everything* young. You consider thirteen early? You consider junior high early?"

"That would've been Mercer, right? You both went to the same junior high, right?"

"I was a year behind her."

"Where'd she go after she left high school?"

"She got a job. My father was dead, my mother . . ."

"Job doing what?"

"Waitressing."

"Where, would you know?"

"A neighborhood restaurant."

"What neighborhood?"

"The Laurelwood section of Riverhead."

"That where you were living at the time?"

"That's where."

"Remember the name of the restaurant?"

"Sure. Rocco's."

"What'd *you* do after high school?"

"I went to jail."

The detectives looked at each other.

"I was sixteen when I took my first fall."

"What for?"

"Aggravated assault. I've been in and out all my life. Fifty-four years old, if I spent twenty of those years on the outside, that's a lot."

"Tell us some more about these friends of your sister's."

"Go ask her husbands," Hendricks said.

Kling was hovering.

It was close to eight P.M. and he was still in the squadroom, wandering from the watercooler to the bulletin board, glancing toward Carella's desk, where he was busy rereading his DD reports, trying to make some sense of this damn case. Strolling over to the open bank of windows, Kling looked down into the street at the early evening traffic, shot another covert glance at Carella, walked back to his own desk, began typing, stopped typing, stood up, stretched, started wandering the room again, hovering. Something was on the man's mind, no question.

Carella looked up at the clock.

"I'd better get out of here," he said.

"Me, too," Kling answered, too eagerly, and immediately went to Carella's desk. "How's it going?" he asked.

"Nothing yet," Carella said. "But we're on it."

"Give it time," Kling said.

Idle talk. Not at all what was really on his mind.

"Sure," Carella said.

Both men fell silent. Kling pulled up a chair, sat. "Mind if I ask you something?" he said.

Carella looked across the desk at him.

"I've had a serious argument with Sharyn."

Carella nodded.

"I thought she was running around behind my back. Turned out she and this colleague, handsome black doctor, were trying to help *another* colleague, a woman who . . . well, it's a long story."

"What was the argument about?"

"Sharyn thinks I betrayed her."

"How?"

"By following her. By not trusting her."

Carella nodded again.

"You agree with her, huh?"

"I've never followed Teddy in my life. Never will."

"Yeah," Kling said. "But I thought . . ."

"*Whatever* you thought."

"Yeah."

They were silent for another moment.

"She doesn't want me to call her."

"So don't."

"For a while, anyway."

"Is that what she said?"

"Yes."

"Well, that's a good sign."

He was thinking, Man, you don't tail a woman you love.

"I want this to work," Kling said.

"Then make sure it does," Carella said.

"I love her, Steve."

"Tell her."

Again and again and again, he thought.

"When do you think I should call her again?"

"Was me?"

"Yeah?"

"I'd call her every minute of every hour of every day until she knew how much I loved her."

"I'm afraid she'll . . ."

He shook his head.

"I'm afraid I'll lose her," he said.

"Tell her."

Kling nodded.

He was already trying to think what he might say the next time he phoned.

Ollie Weeks was still thinking about last Friday night. The dinner with Patricia and her family. Or, more accurately, what had happened in the parking lot after dinner. That was almost a week ago, and all he could do was still think about Patricia Gomez.

To tell the truth, he was beginning to feel a bit conflicted, so to speak. This was probably because Patricia had kissed him good night on the lips. This after her brother had clapped him on the shoulder and said, "You got cool chops, dude." Meaning the way he played piano. This after her father had told him, "I like a man with a hearty appetite." Meaning the way he ate.

Ollie had told Patricia she didn't have to come downstairs with him, it was late, and she'd said, "Hey, I'm a cop." Took the elevator down with him, the hallways and the elevator doors all covered with graffiti, salsa music coming from inside all the apartments. Walked him to his car, and kissed him before he even unlocked the door. On the lips. With her mouth open. And her tongue working.

Which was why he felt so conflicted, so to speak, this Monday evening, when he was about to call Patricia to propose a quiet little dinner alone in his apartment, which he himself would prepare.

Was he merely out to lay Patricia Gomez?

Or was this something more serious, God forbid?

He wished he had someone he could discuss this with.

He wished he knew Steve Carella better.

Only other person he could think of was Andy Parker.

The two men met for a drink at nine that night. Parker suspected something was on Ollie's mind, but he couldn't imagine what it was until Ollie began talking about this great

Spanish dinner he'd had last week up Patricia Gomez's house.

"You still seeing her, huh?" Parker said.

"Well, yeah, every now and then," Ollie said.

"Is that why you're on this diet of yours?"

"What diet?" Ollie asked.

"Or maybe not, a Spanish dinner."

"Patricia says it's okay to go off it every now and then."

"So it was her idea, is that right?"

"No, no, her idea. Come on."

"Then whose idea was it, if not hers? If she's the one can say it's okay to stay on it or go off it, then whose idea was it? The Pope's?"

"So we talked about me losing a few pounds, so what?"

"Looks to me like you lost a lot more than a few pounds. I hardly recognized you when you walked in here."

"Really?" Ollie said, pleased.

"You gotta be careful, losing so much weight so fast."

"Ten pounds is all," Ollie said.

"That's a lot. She must have some grip on you, this girl."

"Naw, come on, whattya mean, grip. Come on. We just see each other every now and then."

"So long as it's just that," Parker said, and nodded emphatically. "You drinking beer cause of the diet?"

"Well, hard liquor has a lot of empty calories," Ollie explained.

"You want another beer?"

"I'm okay with this," Ollie said.

"I'll have another scotch, if it won't offend you, that is."

"Why should it offend me?" Ollie said.

"Who knows, these days?" Parker said, and signaled for a refill and then gulped it down in almost a single swallow. "You hear the one about the Caddys?" he asked.

"Which one is that?"

"If a white man driving a white Caddy is white power," Parker said, "and two black men driving a black Caddy is black power . . ." He grinned in anticipation. "What's three Puerto Ricans driving a maroon Caddy?"

"Puerto Rican power?" Ollie guessed.

"Grand Theft, Auto," Parker said, and burst out laughing.

Ollie nodded, sipped at his beer.

"What'sa matter?" Parker asked.

"Nothing. Why? What'sa matter?"

"You din't think that was funny?"

"Not very."

"Grand Theft, Auto? You din't think that was funny?"

"I thought it was Grand Theft, Auto, is what I thought it was. It coulda been any three guys driving the car, that woulda been Grand Theft, Auto, if they stole the car."

"Yeah, but these were three *spics,* which is what made it Grand Theft, Auto, which is what makes the joke funny."

"Okay, so it's funny," Ollie said. "Ha ha."

"You know what's wrong with you all at once?" Parker said, and jabbed his finger across the table at him.

"I didn't realize anything was wrong with me all at once," Ollie said.

"Yes, all at once you are losing your you-ness."

"My what?"

"Your essential *Ollie*-ness."

"And what is that, my essential Ollie-ness?"

"Your capacity to laugh at niggers and spics and wops and kikes . . ."

"I told you 'ha ha,' didn't I?"

"Yes, but you didn't mean it. You are losing your *ris de veau.*"

"My what?"

"Your *ris de veau.* That's French for 'joy of living.' When the French say a person has *ris de veau,* it means he enjoys life."

"Too bad I ain't French."

"I got another story to tell you," Parker said.

"What's this one?" Ollie said. "Four Jews in a blue Caddy?"

"No, it's about this puppy dog walking along the railroad tracks . . ."

"Is he white, black, or Puerto Rican?"

"He is a little white puppy dog, and this train comes along, and the wheels run over his tail, and he loses the end of his tail. And he's very sad about this. So he puts his head down on the tracks and he begins crying his heart out, and not paying any attention. And just then another train comes along, and runs him over again, cutting off his head this time. You know the moral of that story, Ollie?"

"No, what's the moral?"

"Never lose your head over a piece of tail."

The table went silent.

"You understand me?" Parker said.

Ollie figured maybe this hadn't been such a good idea, after all.

3.

They found the first of Alicia's husbands in a salsa club called Loco Tapas y Vargas on Verglas Street, downtown on the edge of the city's Garment District. Ricky Montero was playing trumpet in one of the club's two "top-name Big Band Orchestras"; neither Parker nor Genero had ever heard of either of them.

Montero's band was rehearsing when they came in at ten thirty that Tuesday morning, the twenty-second day of June. He explained that both bands played mambo, cha-cha, rumba, son, merengue, guaracha, timba, and songo. He told them each of the bands played both "On Two" and "On One" music . . .

"On Two is a mambo style where the break step . . ."

"The what step?"

"The first long step, the break step, comes on the second beat. No pauses."

"Uh-huh."

"With On One, the break comes on the first beat . . ."

"Uh-huh."

". . . and the dancers pause on the fourth and the eighth beats."

Parker nodded.

So did Genero.

Neither knew what the hell Montero was talking about.

"Many dancers prefer the On One style."

"I can see why," Parker said.

"On Two is based on percussion," Montero explained. "Not like On One."

"What's On One based on?"

"Melody."

"Right," Genero said.

Parker felt like ordering a beer. So did Genero.

"Tell us about your ex-wife," Parker said.

"Somebody offed her, huh?" Montero said. "I read about it in the papers. Some kind of serial killer, huh?"

"Well, we don't know that yet."

"All we know so far is she was sexually promiscuous at an early age."

"Well, I wouldn't say that."

"You had no reason to believe that?"

"Well, she had a healthy appetite, let's say."

"For sex, right?"

"Well, sex, yes."

"Which means she was sexually promiscuous, right?"

"Depends on how you define promiscuous."

"How do you define it, Mr. Montero?"

"Well, yes, she was sexually promiscuous, I would say, yes."

"How about drugs? Was she using drugs?"

"Well."

"Because we understand you yourself do . . ."

"No, no."

". . . a little dope."

"No, that's not true. Long ago, maybe. Not no more."

"How long ago?"

"Ten years? When we were together, yes, we experimented a little, you might say."

"With what? Crack?"

"No, no, crack was on the scene much earlier, the crack rage. Alicia and I split ten years ago. Heroin was back by then. All we did was a little shit every now and then."

"Just dabbled, would you say?"

"Oh, yes, nothing serious."

"Not even little teeny-weeny chickenshit habits?"

"No habits at all. Nothing. Like you said, we just dabbled."

"Who helped you with all this dabbling?"

"Not *all* this dabbling. Come on. It was just every now and then. Recreational, you might say. Recreational use. Hey, I'm a musician."

"Alicia wasn't a musician, though."

"Well, we were married. Look, this wasn't such a big deal. Don't try to make it into such a big deal."

"Was she working when you were married?"

"Yes."

"Doing what?"

"Manicuring."

"Would you remember where?"

"No. This was before she got into selling beauty products."

"Why'd you divorce her, Ricky?"

"I didn't."

The detectives looked at him blankly.

"She was the one wanted the divorce."

"Why?"

"Different lifestyles, she said."

"Dope?" Genero said.

"No, we were both experimenting along those lines."

"Sex?"

"I didn't mind that."

"Then what?"

"I have no idea. She just said our lifestyles were too different."

"About this experimenting . . ."

"Just a little."

"Just a little shmeck every now and then, right?"

"Right."

"Who supplied you?"

"Shit, man, you can score on any street corner in this city, don't you know that? I mean, you're cops, you don't know that?"

"Nobody in particular? No favorite dealer?"

"Nobody I'd remember."

"Would you know if she kept on using? After you split?"

"I haven't seen her in ten years."

"So you wouldn't know if she was still 'dabbling'?"

"'Experimenting'?"

"How would I know?"

"But *if* she was . . ."

"I don't know what she . . ."

". . . you wouldn't know who might have been supplying her nowadays."

"I wouldn't know anything about her. I just told you, I haven't seen her in ten years."

"Wouldn't know if she owed some dealer money, for example?"

"Is there a problem with the sound in here? What is it you don't understand? I haven't *seen* the woman in ten years. I don't know if she was shooting dope in her arm or in her eye or even up her ass."

"How do you know she was selling beauty products?"

"Huh?"

"If you haven't seen her in ten years, how do you happen to know that?"

"I heard around."

"From who?"

"I forget who told me. She was selling nail polish and shit. Was what I heard. She was like a sales rep, is what they call it. Look, if you got any more questions, make it fast, okay? I gotta get back on the stand."

"Where were you last Friday night at eight o'clock?"

"Right here. On Fridays I play here from eight at night to two in the morning."

He looked Parker dead in the eye.

"Anything else?" he asked.

Parker took that to mean Good-bye.

The two detectives from Narcotics thought dope was what made the world go round. They were convinced that 9/11 was all about dope. So was the Iraq War. Everything had to do with dope. If we really wanted to end the war on terrorism, if in fact we wanted to end all wars, for all time, then all we had to do was win the war on dope. Dope was evil. Dope dealers were evil. Even people who *used* dope were evil. This is why they had no sympathy for the sixteen-year-old girl who'd dropped dead from an overdose of Angel Dust in the alley outside Ninotchka.

"She had it coming," Brancusi said.

He was the bigger of the two Narcotics dicks. You would not want to struggle with this man over a dime bag of shit.

"You know what Angel Dust is?" his partner said.

As tall as Brancusi, but not as broad in the shoulders or thick in the middle. Irishman named Mickey Connors. Meyer and Carella sensed a bit of condescension here; they both knew what Angel Dust was.

"Angel Dust is phencyclidine," Connors explained.

"PCP," Brancusi further elucidated.

"It's also called crystal, hog, or tic."

"You forgot zoot," Meyer said.

"Are we wasting our time with these guys?" Connors asked his partner.

"No, go ahead, enlighten us," Meyer said.

"Go to hell," Connors said. "Let's go, Benny."

"Stick around," Carella advised. "We're talking a pair of homicides here."

"What is that supposed to do, the word 'homicide'?"

Brancusi asked. "Make us wet our pants? You know how many drug-related murders we see every day of the week?"

"That's why we're here," Carella said.

"Yeah, why *are* you here?" Connors asked.

"Drug-related. Two of our vics may have been users. And one of them was killed outside the club where you guys caught a sixteen-year-old who overdosed on the peace pill."

"Her own hard luck," Connors said.

"Also, the manager of Ninotchka took a fall for dealing ten years ago. So we've got a dead duster and now another vic outside the same club, who may or may not have been using, and the manager once dealt dope, so maybe there's a connection, hmm? So we want to know all about this girl."

"Naomi Maines," Brancusi said.

"She walked out of a club up the street, disassociating, that's for sure, maybe hallucinating, too . . ."

"Then La Paglia was giving us the straight goods."

"Who's La Paglia?" Brancusi asked.

"Manager of Ninotchka. The ex-con."

"Oh yeah, him," Brancusi said, remembering. "A scumbag."

"Told us the girl just wandered by Ninotchka. We think she may have walked over from the other club," Meyer said.

"Yeah, that checks out," Connors said. "Her sister and a girlfriend told us she dropped two tabs of dust inside there."

"That'll do it, all right," Brancusi said.

"Must've started convulsing as she came up the alley, dropped dead outside Ninotchka, the garbage cans out back there."

"Just stopped breathing," Brancusi said.

"What's this other club called?" Meyer asked.

"Grandma's Bloomers."

"Cute."

"Clean, too. Naomi didn't buy the stuff in there, that's for sure."

There was a time not too long ago—five years? ten years?—when this stretch of turf was lined with rave clubs. These nocturnal dance clubs were characterized by pulsating, deafening, techno (or so-called "house") music, blinking strobes, dazzling laser lights, and . . . oh yes . . . club drugs like Ecstasy, ephedrine, ketamine, GHB, methcathinone, LSD, magic mushrooms, methamphetamine, and—well, you name it, we've got it. A crusading mayor padlocked these rave joints all over the city, and the party scene today was a lot milder than it was back then: new mayor, new definition of what was bad for the health; as for example, smoking.

On Austin Street today, only two clubs remained: Ninotchka, dedicated to geriatric lovers of violin music, and Grandma's Bloomers, a 30,000-square-foot space that used to be called The Black Pit when it attracted thirteen- to twenty-year-old ravers, lo, those many years ago. The manager of GB's, as it was familiarly called, was a man named Alex Coombes. Pronounced it "combs," like what you use in your hair. He was in his forties, looked like the kind of father you'd want if you were about to ask for the use of the family car. Gentle brown eyes. Pleasant features. Nice smile. All-around good guy. But a sixteen-year-old had dropped two tabs of Angel Dust in his club six months ago.

"I don't even know how she got *in* here," Coombes said. "Our strict policy is no admission unless you're twenty-one or over. We card at the door, search bags and bodies. No drugs in here. Not then, not now."

Now was eleven fifteen on the morning of June twenty-second. Connors and Brancusi had given them Coombes's home phone number, and he'd agreed to meet them at the club.

"Was that your policy six months ago?" Meyer asked. "Twenty-one or over?"

"It's been our policy *always.* In fact, nowadays the average age is even older than that. Late twenties, early thirties, a nice eclectic mix of straights, gays, and who-can-tell-whats. Two or three months ago, our DJs were spinning techno, reggae, and hip-hop, but now they're moving more toward funkier stuff like the Rolling Stones, T-Rex, MC5, Iggy and the Stooges, all that. We sell alcoholic bevs, yes, mostly exotic, cutesy-poo drinks this age group seems to favor. But drugs? Nossir. Never. I can absolutely guarantee that Naomi Maines did not buy that dust here at GB's. Nossir."

"We think she swallowed two tabs of it in here."

"You think wrong. I just told you. We don't sell . . ."

"Did you *see* her that night?"

"Not that I would know."

"What does that mean?"

"It means if she was here, if she somehow got past the door with a phony ID, I wasn't aware of her."

"Would she have left the club at any time that night?" Meyer asked.

"She might have," Coombes said. "I wouldn't know."

"Who *would* know?"

"Al. Bouncer at the back door. Aldo Mancino. He'd have stamped her hand."

"Is he here now?"

"This is a *night*club," Coombes said. "He doesn't come in till nine tonight. If you want to come back then . . ."

"No, we want his home address," Carella said.

Aldo Mancino's landlady told them he usually went over to "the club" this time of day. The club was the Italian American Club on Dorsey Street all the way downtown. This was now one in the afternoon. Mancino and some other men were sitting outside at round tables, enjoying the rest of this mild day, drinking espresso from the coffee bar next door. Inside the club, Carella could see a television set going, some men shooting pool.

Mancino fit the description his landlady had given them. Big and burly, thirty years old or so, with dark curly hair, bushy eyebrows, and brown eyes, he sat in a tank-top undershirt and blue jeans, muscles bulging, grinning as he delivered the punch line to a joke. The two men with him burst out laughing, then stopped abruptly when they saw Carella and Meyer approaching.

"Mr. Mancino?" Carella said.

Mancino looked up at him.

"Detective Carella," he said, and showed his shield. "My partner, Detective Meyer. Few questions we'd like to ask, if you can spare the time."

"Uh-oh, what'd you do now, Aldo?" one of the other men asked.

"I guess I'm about to find out," Mancino said, and grinned. He had an engaging grin. Nice-looking man altogether.

Couldn't have been anything but a furniture mover or a bouncer. He knew he wasn't in any trouble here; his manner was relaxed and receptive.

"Gentlemen?" Meyer said.

"I guess he's saying this is private," the same man said.

"We won't be long," Carella said.

Both men rose. One of them clapped Mancino on the shoulder. "Let us know where we can bring cigarettes," he said.

"Yeah, yeah," Mancino said.

The two men went inside the club. Carella and Meyer took their empty chairs.

"Grandma's Bloomers," Carella said. "Six months ago."

"That again, huh?" Mancino said.

"Sorry, but something's come up."

"Naomi Maines, right? Cause, you know, they talked me deaf, dumb, and blind already. The two Narcotics cops."

"This is a new case."

"What's it got to do with me? I'll tell you just what I told the narcs. Bobby cards everyone at the front door, even if they look old enough. He would've carded her, too."

"Who's Bobby?"

"Bobby Nardello. He screens everybody going in. Admission is free, but you gotta show ID. And he checks bags and pats you down. There's a girl does the girls. Her name is Tracy."

"We understand you're on the back door."

"Right. We don't like a lot of smokers hanging around outside the front of the club. You're not allowed to smoke inside, you know. So we ask them to go out back, in the alley.

I stamp their hands when they leave, check them when they come back in."

"Did Naomi Maines leave the club anytime before her death?"

"Is that a trick question, or what?"

The detectives looked at him.

"Of *course* she left the club. They found her dead up the street, so she *had* to 've left the club, am I right?"

"Before then, we mean."

"I think so. I'm not sure. You know how many people come out of that club for a smoke? The die-hards come out every ten minutes or so, just gotta have that cigarette, you know. I must stamp a hundred hands every night. Maybe more."

"You think you might've stamped Naomi's hand?"

"I think so. They showed me her picture, the narcs. Attractive blonde girl, very mature looking. Meaning great tits. Never would've thought she was only sixteen. Dress cut down to here. No bra."

"So you do remember her."

"I think so. If she's the one. But she didn't immediately reach for a pack of cigarettes, the way most of them do. She just sort of strolled up the alley. Well, lots of them do that, too. The smokers. They light up, take a little stroll, puff their brains out, then come back inside again."

"Up the street toward Ninotchka?" Carella asked.

"Yeah. Well, yeah, in that direction."

"Naomi, I mean. Did *she* head toward Ninotchka?"

"Yeah. If she's the one."

"How long was she gone?"

"You mean, before she came back in again?"

"Yes."

"Ten, fifteen minutes."

"Could you see her all that time?"

"I wasn't looking."

From his cell phone, Carella called Narcotics and asked Brancusi what the sister's name was.

"Her and the friend both," he said.

"I don't know who you're talking about," Brancusi said.

"Naomi Maines. Her sister and her friend. How do we find them?"

"Why do you want them?" Brancusi said. "This is a cold case."

"Not anymore, it isn't," Carella said.

Both girls were checkers at a supermarket called Garden Basket. Naomi Maines used to work there, too. They were on their break now, smoking out back. Meyer wondered if either of them knew that smoking caused cancer.

The sister's name was Fiona Maines. The other girl was Abby Goldman. They were both older than twenty-one. They both knew young Naomi was breaking the law when she used a fake driver's license to get into the club. They also knew it was against the law to send her out looking for some "stimulants," as they called them. But they figured her youth and innocence would attract less attention than if one of the older girls smuggled the stuff in.

They knew they could score here at Grandma's Bloomers. They'd talked to people who'd been here, they knew the place was wide open. The beauty part was they carded you at the door, checked your handbags, patted you down, went through all the routine; it was like you were a terrorist going through airport security. Fiona was surprised they hadn't been asked to take off their shoes.

"But, you know, that's all a show," she said. "When the place was still The Black Pit, they got raided a lot. So now they weren't taking any chances with the law. Two or three visits, the cops saw all the precautions—hell, you aren't even allowed to *smoke* in there—they figured the place was clean, they didn't bother with it anymore."

"Also, there may be a little payoff there, hmm?" Abby suggested, and winked at Carella. "You guys know all about payoffs, don't you?"

"Sure," Carella said, and winked back. "In fact, we're late for a pickup right this minute."

"I believe you," Abby said.

"Don't," Carella said.

"What I'm trying to say," Fiona said, "is once you were inside, all you had to do was ask any of the waiters where you could get something a little stronger than a Maiden Aunt, one of the gin drinks is called, all pink with oranges and cherries, and he'd tell you, 'Ask Al.' So Al is this big guy Aldo at the back door, he stamps your hand when you go out for a smoke, and you hint to him you might be interested in some powder or pills, and he tells you, 'Ask Dom, up the street.'"

"Dominick La Paglia," Meyer said.

"You guessed it," Fiona said.

"Manager of this old fart place," Abby said.

"Ninotchka," Carella said.

"Is the name of it," Abby said, and puffed on her cigarette. "You guys done your homework. Who'd suspect any drug stuff going down there? Naomi goes up the street, talks to a guy at the back door there, tells him Al asked her to ask for Dom. So Dom appears, and takes her inside to this little room where he's got a whole grocery store of goodies. She comes back with the two tabs of dust for herself and a cap of X each for me and Abby."

"Good stuff, too," Fiona said. "Sometimes, they mix a lot of other shit in with it that can kill you. But pure Ecstasy never hurt anybody."

"Pure Angel Dust killed your sister," Carella said.

"Yeah, but nobody done anything about it, did they? You see Aldo in jail? You see Dom in jail? You see them clubs padlocked? We told all this to the two narcs six months ago. You see them doing anything about it?"

"Little payoff there," Abby said, and winked again.

This time they believed her.

"Let's say we have a place that used to be a rave club," Carella said.

"Let's say," Meyer said.

"Lots of drug use going down there."

"No question."

"The Black Pit. And let's say the former mayor closes it down in his crusade . . ."

"Right . . ."

". . . and it reopens as Grandma's Bloomers."

"Squeaky clean."

"Nobody allowed in unless he's twenty-one."

"Cutesy-poo cocktails."

"No dope."

"*Especially* no dope. But let's say the customers might still crave a little taste every now and then."

"Too bad. We don't have any, kids."

"Ah, but maybe we do."

"By George, maybe we do," Meyer said.

"Just see the club just up the street," Carella said. "Where the manager took a fall for possession with intent."

Meyer nodded sagely.

"You think a judge would grant a search warrant?" Carella asked.

"Maybe," Meyer said.

"Have we got probable cause?"

"Maybe."

"Shall we give it a shot?"

"Nothing to lose," Meyer said.

Well now, by golly, who'd have thought they were going to make a drug bust at a hangout for geezers? But when you thought of it, what made more sense than strolling up the alley to a nice clean establishment where the elderly sat holding hands at tables in the dark as violinists strolled and meanwhile at the back door a man who'd been convicted of possession with intent was back at the old candy stand again?

La Paglia said they were out of their minds.

But they were there with a search warrant, you see.

Probable cause.

Sixteen-year-old girl in attendance at Grandma's Bloomers, a club that meticulously IDs anyone seeking entrance, and she later takes a little stroll up the alley to Ninotchka, and yet later is witnessed swallowing two tabs of dust, and then she's found dead outside Ninotchka, now isn't *that* a remarkable coincidence, Your Honor?

Isn't that probable cause for a search warrant, Your Honor?

Petition granted.

So what say you now, Mr. La Paglia?

"I say talk to your pals at Narcotics. They've been here already. They know the score. Talk to them."

"You gonna let us search the premises?" Meyer asked. "Or you gonna give us trouble here?"

La Paglia decided to give them trouble.

He was a big man, not as tall as either Meyer or Carella, but thicker and beefier than either, and he had no intention of going back to jail, especially on charges that might include the death of a sixteen-year-old girl, there was no way anyone was going to put him back in there with all the butt-fuckers, pole-smokers, and peter-gazers. All you had to do was take one look at prison slang, and you figured in a minute that it wasn't a hell of a lot better doing a grip of time here in America than it was doing it over there in Iraq. There was no way anybody was going to send Dominick La Paglia up again, a three-time loser this time, no way in the world!

He came at them like a bull roaring out of the chutes, looking to gore anybody in the ring. They weren't used to this sort of activity. Your uniforms, who were there on the spot when a crime was going down, got into physical combat more often than your detectives, who usually came in after a crime was committed. Neither Carella nor Meyer could remember the last time they'd worked out at the police gym. So here came a guy who weighed two hundred and ten pounds, and who was still in good shape from lifting weights when he was on the inside, a guy who'd been paying off Narcotics, and maybe Street Crime as well, and who felt entitled to a little *protection* here, instead of two starfish assholes waving a search warrant at him. He felt betrayed, and he felt endangered, and besides he felt he had nothing to lose if he could get out of here past these two range queens, so he smashed his fist into Meyer's face, knocking him off balance and back into Carella, who was reaching for his holstered Glock, when he, too, lost balance.

La Paglia kicked Meyer in the balls, dropping him moaning to his knees. He was about to do the same thing to Carella when the Glock popped into view. He kicked Meyer under the chin instead, hoping this would dissuade the other cop, but the gun was level in Carella's hand now, pointing straight at La Paglia's head, and his eyes spoke even before his mouth did, and his eyes said, *I am going to shoot you dead.*

"Freeze!" he yelled.

La Paglia hesitated just another moment. Meyer was lying flat on the floor now. La Paglia brought back his foot to kick him in the head again, just for spite, and then changed his mind when he heard Carella shout, *"Now!"*

He froze.

He half expected the number she'd given him to be a fake one, but lo and behold, there was her voice on the phone.

"Reggie?" he said.

"Who's this, please?"

"Charles."

"Charles?"

"Remember last Thursday night? You and Trish?"

"Oh, right, sure. Hi, Charles."

He still didn't think she remembered him.

"You gave me your phone number, remember?"

"Sure. How you doin, Charles?"

"Fine, thanks. And you?"

"Fine. You're the guy with the shaved head, right?"

"Right."

"Sure, I remember. So what'd you have in mind, Charles?"

"I bought a new car," he said.

"No kidding?"

"I take delivery tomorrow morning."

"Wow," she said, but she didn't sound at all enthusiastic.

"What I thought . . ."

"Yes, Charles?"

"If you were free tomorrow . . ."

"Yes?"

"We could go for a ride in the country, have lunch at some nice little place on the road, come back to the hotel for dinner, and then spend the night together. If that sounds interesting to you, Reggie."

"It does indeed," she said.

"Well then, good," he said, relieved. "Where shall I pick you up?"

"Are you staying at the hotel now?"

"Yes," he said.

"Well, why don't I just meet you there?"

"Fine. Eleven tomorrow morning?"

"That'll be a long day," she said.

"I know."

"*And* night," she said.

"I realize that."

"We don't have to discuss money, do we, Charles?"

"Not unless you want to."

"It's just . . . it'll be all day, and then all night."

"Yes."

"Does five thousand sound high?"

"It sounds fine, Reggie."

"What kind of car did you buy?" she asked.

He wasn't worried about the money running out. There was enough to last till he did what he still had to do. The home equity loan on the house was big enough to carry him through to the end of this. Just barely, the way he was spending, but that's what this was all about, wasn't it? Corrections? Adjustments? Make for himself now the life he should have enjoyed all along? Drive through the countryside with a nineteen-year-old redhead in a leased Jaguar convertible? That's what this was all about, wasn't it?

The look on Alicia's face when he said, "Remember me? Chuck?"

Oh, Jesus, that was almost worth it all, he'd been almost ready to quit right then and there! That priceless look of recognition an instant before he shot her. Recognition, and then pain. The bullets smashing home. A pain deeper than his own, he supposed. He hoped so. And she'd known.

They would all know, because he would make sure they knew. Hi, remember me? Long time no see, right? Bad penny, right? So long, it's been swell t'know ya!

And bam!

Good.

Tomorrow was a school day, and so the surprise birthday party for the twins was an afternoon one, and they were both home by eight that Tuesday night. When Carella came in at nine thirty, April was in the living room with Teddy, still chattering away, her hands moving on the air for her mother to read. Lipstick. High heels. Miniskirt. His thirteen-year-old daughter now. He yelled, "Hi, everybody," went in to where they were both sitting under the imitation Tiffany lamp, signed *Hi, Sweetie,* kissed Teddy, and then kissed his daughter and asked, "How was the party?"

"Cool," April said, "I was just telling Mom."

"Where's Mark?" he asked.

"In his room," April said.

"Everything okay?"

Teddy discreetly rolled her eyes.

Their eyes met. Communicated.

"I'll go say hello," he said. "When's dinner?"

"Mark and me ate at the party," April said.

Mark and I, Teddy signed.

"*You* ate at the party, too?" April said aloud, and then signed it, just in case her mother had missed her dynamite wit. Teddy mouthed *Ha ha.* Carella was already on the way down the hall to his son's room.

Mark was lying on his bed, hands behind his head, staring

up at the ceiling. No music blaring. No TV on. He made room for his father, sat up when his father took the offered space.

"What's the matter?" Carella asked.

Mark shrugged.

"Tough being a teenager?" Carella said, and put his arm around his son's shoulders.

"Dad . . ." Mark said, and hesitated.

"Tell me."

"You know who I always thought was my best friend?"

"Who, son?"

"April. Dad, she's my *twin*! I mean, she was my *womb* mate, excuse me, that's a twelve-year-old joke, I'm thirteen now, I have to stop behaving like a friggen *Munchkin*!"

And suddenly he was in tears.

He buried his face in Carella's shoulder.

"What happened, Mark?"

"She called me and my friends Munchkins!"

"Who did?"

"Lorraine Pierce. The girl who gave the party for us. It's because lots of us are still shorter than the girls, and our voices are beginning to change, but that's no reason to tease us. We're thirteen, *too,* Dad. We have a right to grow up, too!"

"What's this got to do with your sister?"

"April let her! She just laughed along with all the other girls and the older boys. My own sister! My *twin*!"

"I'll talk to her."

"No, let it go, please. They were just showing off."

Mark dried his eyes. Carella kept looking at him.

"What else, son?"

"Nothing."

"Tell me what else."

"Dad . . . I think she's a bad influence."

"Who, son?"

"Lorraine Pierce. April's best friend."

"Because she called you and your friends Munchkins?"

"No, because . . ." He shook his head. "Never mind. I don't want to be a snitch."

"Nothing wrong with snitches, son. Why is she a bad influence, this Lorraine?"

"To begin with, I know she's a shoplifter."

Carella was suddenly all ears.

"How do you know that?"

"April told me."

"How does she know?"

"She was in the drugstore with Lorraine when she swiped a bottle of nail polish."

"When was this?"

"Two, three weeks ago."

"Tell me about it," Carella said, and got up to close the door.

April had already gone down the hall to her room by the time Carella came back into the living room. Teddy was still sitting under the imitation Tiffany, reading, her hands in her lap, her black hair glossy with light. She closed the book at once.

Did he say anything? she signed.

"Plenty," Carella said.

The way Mark reported it to him . . .

Around the beginning of the month sometime, April had gone to a Saturday afternoon movie with her good friend Lorraine Pierce. They'd stopped in a drugstore on the way home, and April was leafing through a copy of *People* magazine, when she saw Lorraine slip a bottle of nail polish into her handbag. At first, she couldn't believe what she was seeing: Lorraine taking a quick glance at the cashier, and then swiftly dropping the bottle into her bag . . .

"Lorraine!" she whispered.

Lorraine turned to her. Blue eyes all wide and innocent.

"Put that back," April whispered.

"Put what back?"

April looked toward where the cashier was checking out a fat woman in a flowered dress. Moving so that she shielded Lorraine from the cashier's view, she whispered, "Put it back. Now."

"Don't be ridic," Lorraine said, and walked out of the store.

On the sidewalk outside, April caught her arm, pulled her to a stop.

"My father's a cop!" she said.

"It's just a stupid bottle of nail polish," Lorraine said.

"But you *stole* it!"

"I buy lots of things in that store."

"What's that got to do with it?"

"I'll pay them when I get my allowance."

"Lorraine, you *stole* that nail polish."

"Don't be such a pisspants," Lorraine said sharply.

They were walking swiftly up the avenue, away from the

drugstore. April felt as if they'd just robbed a bank. People rushing by in either direction, the June heat as thick as yellow fog. The stolen nail polish, the swag, sitting at the bottom of Lorraine's handbag.

"Give it to me, I'll take it back," April said.

"No!"

"Lorraine . . ."

"You're an accomplice," Lorraine said.

Teddy watched Carella's mouth, his flying fingers. At last, she nodded.

They could have both got in serious trouble, she signed.

"That's what Mark told her."

What'd she say to that?

"You don't want to hear it."

I do.

"She repeated Lorraine. She said, 'Don't be such a pisspants.'"

April *said that?*

"I'm sorry, hon."

April?

Teddy sat motionless for a moment.

When she raised her hands again, she signed, *I'll have a talk with her.*

When the phone on Lieutenant Byrnes's desk rang, he thought it was his wife, Harriet, wanting to know why he wasn't home yet. Instead, it was the Chief of Detectives.

"I was wondering how you thought the department should proceed with this case," he told Byrnes. "From now on, that is. The media's having a field day with the blind guy, you know. War hero, all that shit."

"We're okay with it," Byrnes said. "In fact, we just wrapped a drug bust. That's why you caught me here."

"What's a drug bust got to do with two homicides?"

"Long story," Byrnes said.

"It better be a good one," the Chief said. "Cause I have to tell you, I'm thinking your plate might be too full just now . . ."

"We can handle it without a problem," Byrnes said.

"The Commish thinks we may need a display of special attention here, his words. A dead war hero. Blind, no less."

"The Eight-Seven is prepared to give the case all the special attention it needs," Byrnes said.

The two men were negotiating.

If the case got pulled away from the Eight-Seven, the tabloids would make the squad appear incapable of investigating something this big. On the other hand, if the Chief left the case solely to a dinky little precinct in one of the city's backwaters, the tabs would be watching like hawks, waiting for the first mishap.

"The Commish wants a Special Forces man on it at all times," the Chief said at last.

"In what capacity?"

"Advisory and supervisory."

"Riding with my people?"

"At all times."

"No. They'll file with him, but they don't need a third leg."

"He rides with them."

"I told you no."

"We'll call it a joint task force, whatever. Your people and the man from Special Forces."

"And just who might that be?" Byrnes asked, sounding suddenly very Irish and very stubborn.

"Georgie Fitzsimmons," the Chief said.

"*That* prick?" Byrnes said. "No way will I let him ride with any of my people."

"Pete . . ."

"Don't 'Pete' me, Lou. We're not cutting that kind of deal here. Call it what you want to call it, a joint task force, a special task force, but all we do is report back to Fitz at the end of the day, and that's that."

"How long have I known you, Pete?"

"Too long, Lou."

"Do me this favor."

"No. We're on it. It's under control. We'll file with Fitz at the end of the day. That's the deal."

"They'd better come up with something, Pete."

"We're working it, Lou. We just made a goddamn drug bust!"

"Soon," the Chief warned.

"We're working it," Byrnes said again.

4.

In this city there were some 4,000 nail salons scattered hither and yon, most of them in small, modest, fluorescent-lighted spaces in walk-up buildings, some more luxurious, with chandeliers, sculpted vases, silk-embroidered divans, and even stained-glass windows. A tenth of the city's estimated Korean population was employed in these salons, some 50,000 in all, mostly all of them women. An industrious woman could earn as much as a hundred dollars a day, plus tips, giving manicures, pedicures, or—in the fancier establishments—green-tea treatments, Asian foot massages, or painted nail extensions. Moreover, instead of having to stand on her feet all day in a Dunkin' Donuts or a factory, a girl could sit while she worked in one of these nail parlors. It sure beat wading around in a rice paddy.

The woman who owned and operated Lotus Blossom Nails had a rags-to-riches story, and she was not at all reluctant to tell it. Looking like the madam of a whore house in some forties movie set in Shanghai, as loquacious as a Jewish yenta, Jenny Cho—for such was her Americanized name—told the detectives that she'd opened her first salon fifteen years ago, with a $30,000 start-up investment, after a ten-week course that gave her a license in manicuring. Before then, she'd clipped, filed, and polished her own nails at home . . .

"Korean girl have very strong nail," she told them. "No need nail salon. We do for ourselves."

. . . and now she ran a string of six manicure salons scattered all over the city, all with the word "Blossom" in their names. *Yon* had been her Korean name, before she changed it to Jenny. It meant "lotus blossom."

The detectives listened politely.

At ten that Wednesday morning, there were women all over the place, sitting in these high, black-leather upholstered chairs, feet soaking in tubs of water, nails getting painted, or dried, reading magazines. One of the ladies with her feet in a tub was sitting with her skirt pulled up almost to Seoul. Parker was tempted not to look.

"Who you looking for?" Jenny asked.

"Know a woman named Alicia Hendricks?" Parker said.

"Beauty Plus?"

"Lustre Nails?"

"Oh sure," Jenny said. "She come here alla time. Nice girl. She okay?"

"She's dead," Parker said.

Jenny's eyes immediately shifted. Just the very slightest bit, almost as if the light had changed, it was that subtle. But both these men were detectives, and that's why they were here in person, rather than at the other end of a phone. They both saw the faint flicker of recognition; both realized they might be getting close to something here.

Jenny was no fool.

She caught them catching on.

Saw in their eyes the knowledge of what they'd seen in hers.

"I so sorry to hear that," she said, and ducked her head.

They allowed her the moment of grief, authentic or otherwise.

"When did you see her last?" Parker asked.

"Two, t'ree week ago. She come by with new line. What happen to her?"

Sounding genuinely concerned.

"Someone shot her."

"Why?"

You tell us, Parker thought.

"How long did you know her?" Genero asked.

"Oh, maybe two year. T'ree?"

"Did you know she was doing drugs?"

Straight out. Made Alicia sound like a cotton shooter or some other kind of desperate addict, but what the hell. It certainly caught Jenny Cho's attention.

The word flashed in her brown eyes like heat lightning.

She knew Alicia was doing drugs. Dabbling. Experimenting. Whatever. But she knew. And she wanted no part of it now. The alarm sizzled in her eyes, they could feel her backing away from the very word. Drugs. Shrinking away from the knowledge.

But she was smart.

"Yes, but not so much," she said. "Some li'l pot, you know?"

"Uh-huh," Parker said.

"Any idea where she was getting it?" Genero asked.

"You go An'rews Boul'vard, you buy pot anyplace. All over the street, anyplace."

"Uh-huh," Parker said again.

"Other dope, too," Jenny said. "All kine'a heavy shit."

"You think she might've been doing any of the heavier stuff?"

"No," Jenny said. "No, no. She a good girl. Jussa li'l pot ever now and then. Dass all."

The detectives said nothing.

"Ever'body do a li'l pot ever now and then," Jenny said.

They still said nothing.

"Why? You think dass why somebody maybe shoot her?" Jenny said.

"Maybe," Parker said, and shrugged.

"What do you think?" Genero asked.

"I think I so sorry she dead," Jenny said.

"So tell me about yourself," Reggie said.

The top of the Jaguar was down, they were tooling along

soundlessly on back roads, her red hair blowing in the wind. He had bought a billed motoring cap at Gucci's, cost him four hundred dollars, the tan leather as soft as a baby's ass. He wore it tilted jauntily over one eye. All he needed was a pair of goggles to make him look like some kind of Italian playboy.

"What would you like to know?" he asked.

She was wearing a white T-shirt and a green mini. She'd kicked off her flat sandals, and was leaning back in her seat now, her knees bent, the soles of her feet propped up against the glove compartment. The radio was tuned to an easy-listening station, the volume up to combat the rush of wind around the car. It was a bright beautiful day, and she was a bright beautiful girl. He could almost forget she was a hooker.

"Well, for example," she said, "what kind of work do you do?"

"I'm retired," he said.

"What kind of work *did* you do?"

"I was in sales."

"When was this?"

"I left the job just recently."

"Why?"

"Tired of it."

Reggie nodded, brushed hair back from her eyes.

"So what've you been doing since?"

"Loafing."

"For how long?"

"Past few months."

"You can afford to do that?"

"Oh yes."

"I guess *so,*" she said, and giggled, and opened her arms wide to the car. Music oozed from the speakers, swirled around them.

"How old are you, anyway?" she asked.

"Fifty-six," he said.

"Bingo, no hesitation."

"Is that okay?"

"Yeah, I like it. It's called being honest."

"Or foolhardy."

"Fifty-six. You look younger. I guess it's the bald head. How long have you worn it that way?"

"Past few months."

"I like it. Very trendy."

"Thanks."

"You ought to get an earring."

"You think?"

"For the left ear. Right is a signal to fags."

"I didn't know that."

"Sure."

Music swirled around the car, drifted away behind them.

"I'm enjoying this," she said.

"I'm glad."

"I ought to be paying *you,*" she said, and then immediately, "Don't get any ideas!"

They both burst out laughing.

Huntsville, Texas, is about 70 miles north of Houston and 170 miles south of Dallas/Fort Worth. Not for nothing is it known as the "prison city" of Texas: There are eight prisons in Huntsville, and some 15,000 inmates are imprisoned there. This means that every third or fourth citizen of the city is a prison inmate. It further means that the Texas Department of Criminal Justice is the city's biggest employer; only two percent of Huntsville's citizens are out of work.

Walker County prison records showed that Alvin Randolph Dalton was released on parole almost twenty years ago, and subsequently granted permission to move out of state. Parole records here in this city indicated assiduous attendance. He'd paid his debt to society in full, and was now free to go wherever he chose to go, and do whatever he chose to do within the law. But, no longer required to report to anyone anywhere, his whereabouts were a mystery until they checked the phone books, and found a listing for an A. R. Dalton on Inverness Boulevard in Majesta.

A phone call confirmed that he was the man they wanted.

Parker told him to wait there for them.

Dalton said, "What is this?"

Same as Hendricks asked up there in Castleview.

"Just *wait* there," Parker said.

The Walker County prison records gave Dalton's age as fifty-seven. Remarkably fit, jailhouse tattoos all over his bulging muscles, entirely bald and wearing an earring in his right ear, he greeted them in a black tank-top shirt and black jeans, barefooted, and told them at once that Wednesday was his day off. What he did was drive a limo for Intercity Transport, mostly airport pickups and dropoffs, but sometimes trips to the casinos upstate or across the river.

"So what's this about?" he asked.

"Your wife got killed," Genero said.

"I don't have a wife," Dalton said.

"Your former wife. Alicia Hendricks."

"Yeah. Her. That's too bad. What's it got to do with me? I haven't seen her in fifteen years, it must be."

"Lost track of her, is that it?"

Dalton looked at them.

"What is this?" he said again.

"Routine," Genero said.

"Bullshit," Dalton said. "You guys get a dead woman whose ex done time, all at once your ears go up. Well, fellas, I've been clean for almost twenty years now, a gainfully employed, respectable citizen of this fair city. I wouldn't know Alicia if I tripped over her, dead *or* alive. You're barking up the wrong tree."

"How long you been wearing your head bald?" Parker asked.

"Why? Some bald-headed guy do her?"

"How long?"

"My hair began falling out in stir. Before I got busted, I was living in D-Town, wore it long like a hippie. All of a sudden, I'm a white male inmate with a bald head, the hamhocks hung a racist jacket on me, made my life miserable."

"When's the last time you saw Alicia?"

"Whoo. We're talkin fifteen years ago, that's when we got divorced. We're talkin Johnny Carson leaving *The Tonight Show.* We're talkin the invasion of Kuwait. We're talkin the first Gulf War. We're talkin ancient *history,* man!"

"Was she doing dope back then?"

"Who says she was doing dope ever?"

"That's what you went down for, isn't it? A dope violation."

"I learned my lesson."

"*Was* she doing dope?"

"Nothing serious."

"Nothing serious like what?"

"Little griff every now and then."

"And you?"

"Same thing. Marijuana never hurt nobody."

"That right?"

"Marijuana's the most frequently used illegal drug in the United States."

"Tell us all about it, professor."

"Over eighty-three million Americans over the age of twelve have tried marijuana at least once."

"Including Alicia, huh?"

"Big deal."

"She ever move on to the heavier shit?"

"Not to my knowledge. Not while we were married, anyway."

"How about after you split?" Genero said. "You sure she never went hardcore?"

"Is that a trick question, Sherlock? I told you I never saw her after the divorce. Why? You think some dealer did her?"

"We understand she was keeping bad company."

"Not on my watch."

"On your watch, all you did was blast a little stick every now and then, right?"

"That's not all we did."

"Just two happy airheads . . ."

"Don't put the marriage down," Dalton warned. "In many ways, it was a good one."

"In what ways was it a bad one?"

"Why'd you get a divorce?"

Dalton hesitated.

"So?" Parker said.

"She was running around on me."

"But that wasn't bad company, right?"

"It was the company she chose. That didn't mean I had to go along with it."

"Where were you last Friday night at around eight o'clock, Al?"

"Airtight," Dalton said.

"Let's hear it."

"I was driving a van to an Indian casino upstate."

"We suppose you have wit . . ."

"Six of them. All high rollers. Check it out."

The waiter possessed the good grace not to card Reggie. Then he spoiled it by saying, "I'm assuming your daughter is twenty-one."

"Yes," Charles said.

The waiter nodded and padded off.

"Did that bother you?" she asked.

"A little."

"When he comes back, I'll kiss you on the mouth."

"You don't have to."

"You realize there are guys dying in Iraq who can't order a drink in this state?"

"It was that way when I was a kid, too. We used to bitch about it all the time. Being in the Army, not allowed to order a drink."

"What war was that?"

"Vietnam."

"You were in that war?"

"Oh yes."

"Wow," she said. "That seems so long ago."

"To me, too."

"Are you from here originally? I don't mean *here*, this state, I mean the city," and with a jerk of her head indicated its general direction.

"Yes."

"I was born and raised in Denver," she said.

"I've always wanted to go out West."

"Maybe we can go out there together sometime," she said.

"Well . . . maybe. Yes."

"Wouldn't you like to?"

"Here we go," the waiter said, and placed their drinks on the table. "Did you folks want to hear the specials now, or would you like to enjoy your drinks first?"

"Give us a few minutes," he said.

"Take your time," the waiter said, and went off again.

"So you were in the Army, huh?"

"Yes."

"See any action?"

"Yes."

"When did you get out?"

"1970."

"I wasn't even born yet!"

"Shh, he'll hear you."

"Fuck him," she said. "I think I will kiss you on the mouth."

And reached across the table, and cupped his face in her hands, and kissed him openmouthed, her tongue searching.

All of Jenny Cho's salons had the word "Blossom" in their names. Plum Blossom—where the detectives were now headed—Peony Blossom, Pear Blossom, Cherry Blossom, Apricot Blossom, and the eponymous flagship establishment Jenny herself ran, Lotus Blossom. It would have been simpler to call each and every one of these places to ask questions about Alicia Hendricks. But Genero and Parker were still pursuing the "drug-related" angle, and were trying to find out whether her supplier—if indeed such a supplier existed—might be someone she'd met at any of the regular stops on her schedule. Besides, you couldn't gauge reaction on the telephone; that's why legwork was invented. That's why it took so much time to track down a person's story. In police work, everyone had a story. Was Alicia's story dope? Getting the story straight was often the answer to solving a crime.

The first thing the manager of Plum Blossom Nails said to Parker was, "Pedicue ten dollah ex'ra."

He was pointing at Parker's shoes.

The two detectives had barely set foot in the shop, guy tells Parker it's ten dollars extra. He looked down at his feet.

"I don't want a pedicure," he said.

"Manicue same price," the manager said. "Pedicue ten dollah ex'ra."

"I don't want a manicure, either," Parker said. "Why is it ten dollars extra for a pedicure?" He was thinking of busting this little bald-headed gook for price gouging or something.

"You man," the manager said. "Big feet."

"But you save on nail polish," Parker said.

"Big feet," the manager insisted, shaking his head. "Ten dollah ex'ra."

"That's sexist," Genero said.

"Exactly," Parker said. "If this was a man's barbershop, and you charged a woman ten dollars extra for a pedicure, she'd take a feminist fit. Am I right, ladies?" he asked, playing to the house now, hoping for a little female support here.

"Right on, brother," one of the women shouted, and thrust her clenched fist at the air. The others kept reading their magazines.

"I feel like getting a pedicure just for the hell of it," Parker said. "Make this a test case."

"Sure," the manager agreed. "But ten dollah ex'ra."

"You in charge here?" Genero asked, and showed his shield.

"Why, wassa motta?" the manager asked.

"We're investigating a murder," Parker said, using the word "murder" instead of "homicide," which they probably didn't understand in Korea. Scare the shit out of the little gook, he was thinking. Ten dollars extra for a fuckin pedicure! "Does the name Alicia Hendricks mean anything to you?"

The manager looked at him blankly.

But he was scared now. Fear in his eyes. Well, sure, a murder investigation.

"Works for Beauty Plus," Genero said.

"Lustre Nails," Parker said.

"She'd have come here selling nail polish, cuticle remover, nail hardener, all that related stuff. A sales rep."

"Ring a bell?"

The manager was shaking his head.

"We're trying to work up her story."

"Find out who might've wanted her dead."

"Remember her?"

Still shaking his little bald head. Eyes wide in fright. Well, murder.

"You're not in any trouble here," Genero assured him. "This is like a background check."

"Alicia Hendricks," Parker said.

"Nobody," the manager said, shaking his head. "No. On'y Korean girl work here."

In the car on the way to Pear Blossom Nails, Parker asked, "Who said she *worked* there? Did anybody tell him she worked there?"

"No, we told him she was a sales rep."

"And who said she *wasn't* Korean?"

"What do you mean?"

"Did anybody say Alicia Hendricks wasn't Korean?"

"Well, no, but the name . . ."

"They all take American names. You ask any of the Korean girls in there what their names are, they'll tell you Mary or Terry or Kelly or Cathy or whatever. So why couldn't *Alicia* be Korean?"

"Well, Hendricks. That don't sound Korean."

"She could be married to an American. Nice Korean girl married to an American, why not? My point is, what made that little bald-headed jerk think she wasn't Korean? Ten dollars extra, can you imagine that?"

"You think he knew her, is that it?"

"I got no idea he knew her or he didn't know her. Of *course* he knew her! She goes there all the time to sell her nail polish, she's a regular like Clairol or Revlon, all at once he never heard of her! Tells us all the girls in there are Korean, when nobody said she *wasn't* Korean!"

"You think he's hiding something?"

"He better not be," Parker said.

Because she couldn't drive and sign at the same time, Teddy pulled the car into a roadside Starbucks, and talked to her daughter over lattes. This was after April's Wednesday afternoon ballet lesson; she was sweaty and sticky and wasn't expecting an ambush.

"Who told you that?" she asked at once.

Mark, Teddy signed.

"I'll kill him!"

No, you won't kill anyone. He did the right thing.

They were sitting almost knee to knee on the front seat, mother and daughter, facing each other, look-alikes. Teddy's latte was in the cup holder, April's in her right hand.

Why didn't you tell me yourself? Teddy asked.

April said nothing.

April?

"I couldn't tell *anyone,* Mom. That was the thing of it. Not you, not even Mark at first. And I can just *imagine* what Dad's reaction would've been if I casually mentioned that Lorraine Pierce had shoplifted a five-dollar bottle of red Revlon Crayon polish #34 from the local drugstore! Mr. Morality himself? Break out the handcuffs!"

He'd have done no such thing! And you know it!

"Well, I wasn't sure. The other thing was . . . Lorraine's my very best friend on earth. We sit together in every class in school, spend all our free time together, do things together, talk about things together, *secret* things . . . we're like *sisters,* you know? It was like forget the petty bullshit, Ape, what's a little bottle of nail polish between friends to the end?"

Teddy said nothing about her language.

Or that someone was calling her daughter Ape.

"It was really difficult, Mom," April said. "Really."

I want you to promise me something, Teddy signed.

"Mom, please don't ask me to stop seeing Lorraine."

No, I won't do that. But if anything like this ever happens again . . .

"I promise," April said.

You'll tell your father or me right away.

"Yes, I promise," April said.

The word was out. No question about it. If the reaction at Plum Blossom was merely a harbinger, the responses at Pear Blossom and then Apricot Blossom were clear indications that nobody was about to tell them anything much about Alicia Hendricks.

This wasn't quite the "Nobody Knows Nothing" stonewalling you got in the Eight-Seven hood, or even in Washington, D.C., for that matter; the managers of the Blossom shops couldn't very well deny the existence of a woman who visited them regularly to promote and sell Beauty Plus's line of nail-care products. Instead, they all nodded and bowed and smiled in the Oriental manner, oh yes, we know Alicia, oh yes, she very nice girl, come here alla time, we buy many nail polish from her, oh, she dead? So sorry to hear. Nice girl.

But mention dope . . .

Fortified by the La Paglia drug bust yesterday, they were still pursuing the drug-related angle . . .

. . . and immediately the faces went blank.

Dope was news to all of them.

Except to Jenny Cho, of course, who had admitted that Alicia did "Some li'l pot, you know?"

But that was earlier today, and this was now, and the word had gone out, and the party line had changed.

Drug use?

Alicia?

No, no. Smiling. Bowing. Ladies all over the place looking up when the detectives mentioned drugs. This couldn't be too good for business, all these nice city-slick ladies with their smooth sleek legs and their skirts pulled up over their thighs, hearing the word "drugs" bandied about as if this was some street corner near a playground someplace instead of a civilized establishment where you could even get a bikini wax. What was the world coming to?

The world was coming to a dead end.

Until they visited a place called Cherry Blossom Nails.

They knew the minute they stepped through the doorway that they weren't supposed to be here to witness whatever was going down. There was that silent electric buzz that indicated something illegal was happening here. Eyes flashing. People caught in the act, though all that seemed to be happening was innocent manicures and pedicures. They flashed tin simultaneously, and marched straight to the back of the shop, the manager rushing along behind them, waving her hands in the air, yelling that a waxing was in progress, and then turning abruptly and running for the front of the shop when she saw they were about to open one of two closed doors in a narrow passageway.

Genero ran after her.

Parker threw open the door.

A small Asian man was sitting behind a small table upon which rested what appeared to be a one-kilo brick of cocaine.

The detectives had just stepped in shit, as the saying goes.

On the drive back to the city, he told her what the options for this evening were.

"I have an errand to run," he said. "We can either have dinner before or after, take your choice."

"What kind of errand?"

"Someone I have to see."

"I'm not hungry yet, are you?"

"No."

"So why don't we make it a late dinner?"

"Good. You can wait for me at the hotel."

"What time will you be leaving?"

"Around seven."

"I'll take a little nap."

"Okay," he said.

"What time will you be back?"

"Eight, eight thirty."

"Will we be going out?"

"Absolutely. Celebrate."

"Oh? What?"

"Us," he said.

Jenny Cho told them Alicia was nothing but a mew.

They didn't know what she meant at first.

She was trying to say that no one would have killed her for her minor role in what amounted to a penny-ante drug operation.

"She on'y a mew," Jenny insisted.

They finally realized she was telling them Alicia was "only a mule." No, not a so-called swallower, who ingested drugs packed into latex gloves in order to transport the contraband through customs, not that kind of mule. Nor even a so-called stuffer, who inserted similarly packed drugs into vagina or anus with the same end in mind, you should pardon the pun. Just your everyday, garden-variety mule, a mere delivery boy, or girl in this case, woman actually, because she'd been fifty-five years old, even though Jenny Cho called her a delivery boy, a mew, a mule.

Jenny would not tell them the source of the cocaine Alicia delivered to her Blossom salons on her regularly scheduled visits. Jenny knew that in the business of drug trafficking or distribution, there were worse things than arrest and imprisonment. A garrulous person could oftimes meet with a sudden and untimely demise. But she did not think Alicia's death had anything to do with her activities as a courier. She was "ony smaw potatoes," she said. "A deli'ry boy. A mew."

The bust itself was small potatoes.

This wasn't the French Connection, or even the Pizza Connection. This wasn't billions of dollars of heroin or cocaine being smuggled into the United States with the illegal proceeds being laundered via many different methods and through many different countries. This was merely a Korean immigrant, a self-made woman in a land of opportunity, an enterprising woman who'd seen a way to earn a few extra bucks by funneling dope through her shops, which was safer and more convenient, after all, than having to buy it "all over the street, anyplace."

Her arrest put an end to her success story.

But it left open the question of who had murdered Alicia Hendricks and Max Sobolov.

The campus lights were spaced some twenty feet apart. This meant that there were pools of illumination under each lamppost, and then stretches of utter darkness, and then another splash of light as the path meandered its way between buildings and benches toward the sidewalk and the nighttime city beyond.

Christine Langston had packed the papers for the spot test she'd administered during her three o'clock class on the Romantic Poets, and was heading off campus, matching her stride to the areas of darkness and light, making a game of it, bulging briefcase swinging in her right hand. She was a woman in her late sixties, but spry as a goat, as she was fond of saying, and alert to every nuance of campus sound. This was the middle of June, and the cicadas were at it hot and heavy, as were the students, she suspected, mating behind and on top of every errant blade of grass.

In the far distance, she could see the beckoning street lamps on Hall Avenue. She would catch an express bus there, and be whisked downtown to her apartment in sixteen minutes flat. Mortimer would be waiting there for her, mixed drink ready, dinner heating in the kitchen. She would report to him on her day, and listen to his publishing-industry atrocity stories, and then they would have their dinner and perhaps go down for a stroll later on, walking hand in hand in the quiet streets outside the apartment they shared. And yet later, they would . . .

"Professor Langston?" the voice said.

She had just stepped into the circle of light under one of the lampposts. Peering into the darkness beyond, she asked, "Who is it?"

"Me," he said. "Chuck."

And shot her twice in the face.

5.

Mortimer Shea was wearing a bulky cardigan sweater with a shawl collar. He was smoking a pipe. He was bald except for a halo of hair above and around his ears and the back of his head. A manuscript sat on the desk before him in his corner office at Armitage Books. The place seemed Dickensian to Kling and Brown, but they'd never been inside a publishing house before. Shea's title here was Publisher.

There were also two framed photographs on his desk. One showed a rather horse-faced young woman, the other showed a similarly horse-faced older woman. It took the detectives a moment to realize they were not mother and daughter, but instead the same unattractive woman at different stages of her life.

"Christine," Shea informed them. "The one on the left was taken while she was still in college. The other only last summer. But there's the same vibrant love of life in each photo."

"Got any idea who might've wished her harm?" Brown asked. Standing there big and black and scowling, he sounded and looked as if he might be accusing Shea of the crime; actually, he simply wanted to know if Christine Langston had any enemies that Shea knew of.

"At any university, there are interdepartmental jealousies, rivalries. But I sincerely doubt any of Christine's colleagues could have done something like this."

How about *you*? Kling wondered.

Shea was a man in his early seventies, still robust, clear-eyed. The super of his building had told them the lady—meaning Christine—had moved in with him around Christmastime. The super said they seemed like a nice couple.

"How long did you know her?" Kling asked.

"I met her four years ago. We published a book of hers. I edited it."

"What sort of book?"

"An appreciation of Byron." Shea paused. "Do you know who I mean?"

"Yes," Kling said.

"You'd be surprised how many people don't know who Byron was. Or Shakespeare, for that matter. In one of her classes last week, Christine asked her students if they were familiar with the words, 'To be or not to be.' Christine asked them to identify the source, and extend the quotation if they could. Eight students in the class. What would you guess their answers were?"

The detectives waited.

"Four of the eight couldn't identify the source at all. Three of them said the source was *Hamlet.* The eighth said *Romeo and Juliet.* Six people couldn't extend the quotation at all. Two people could add only, 'That is the question.' One student told her after class that it would have been a lot easier if Christine had given them a quote from a *movie.* 'To be or not to be,' can you imagine? Only the greatest soliloquy ever written for the English-speaking stage!" Shea shook his head in despair. "Sometimes, she would come home weeping."

"When did you start living together?" Kling asked.

"Well, almost immediately. That is to say, we kept our own apartments, but de facto we were living together. She didn't give up her place and move in with me until last Christmas."

"When's the last time you saw her alive, Mr. Shea?" Brown asked.

"Yesterday morning. When she left for work. We had breakfast together and then . . . she was gone."

"What were you doing last night around eight o'clock?" Kling asked.

Shea said nothing for a moment. Then he said, "Is this the scene where I ask if I'm a suspect?"

"This isn't a scene, sir," Kling said.

"I was here in the office. Working on this very manuscript," Shea said, and lightly tapped the pages on his desk. "Dreadful, I might add."

"Anyone here with you?"

"Any number of people. We work late in publishing."

"What my partner means . . ."

"Did anyone *see* me here? I believe Freddie Anders stopped in at one point. You might ask him to corroborate. His office is just down the hall."

"What time was that? When he stopped in?"

"I believe it was around six thirty, seven."

"Anyone see you here at *eight,* Mr. Shea?"

"Oh dear. Now we have the scene where I ask if I need a lawyer, isn't that right?"

"You don't need any lawyer," Brown said. "We have to ask these questions."

"I'm sure," Shea said. "But to set the record straight, I didn't leave here until ten last night. When I got to the apartment, the police were already there, informing me that Christine had been shot and killed. For your information, I loved her enormously. In fact, we planned to be married in the fall. I had no reason to kill her, and I did not kill her. And now, if you don't mind, I'd like you to leave."

"Thanks for your time," Kling said.

Shea turned back to the manuscript on his desk.

"Everybody's always innocent," Brown said. "Nobody ever did anything. Catch 'em with the bloody hatchet in their hands, they say, 'This ain't my hatchet, this is my uncle's hatchet.' Wonder anybody's in jail at all, so many innocent people around."

"You think he was lying?" Kling asked.

"Actually, I think he was telling the truth. But he had no reason to get all huffy that way. We *do* have to ask the goddamn questions."

The car's air conditioner wasn't working, and the windows, front and back, were wide open. The noonday traffic sounds were deafening, discouraging conversation. They rode in silence, in stifling heat.

"Artie," Kling said at last, "I got a problem."

Brown turned from the wheel to look at him. Kling kept staring straight ahead through the windshield.

"I think Sharyn and I may be breaking up," he said.

His last words were almost lost in the baffle of city traffic. Brown always looked as if he were scowling, but this time he really was. He turned to Kling again, briefly, scowling in reprimand, or disbelief, or merely because he wasn't sure he had heard him correctly.

"I thought she was cheating on me," Kling said. "I followed her."

"She'd never cheat on you in a million years, man."

"I know that."

"So what the hell's wrong with you? You go tailin the woman you love?"

"I know."

"Playin cops and robbers, the woman you love."

"I know."

"Where's this at now? Where'd you leave it?"

"She doesn't want to talk yet. She says I hurt her too much."

"Yeah, well, you did! I ever go followin Caroline, she'd put me in the hospital."

"I know."

Brown was shaking his head now. "Big detective, what's *wrong* with you, man?"

"She thinks . . . Artie, can I say this?"

"How do I know what you're gonna say before you say it?"

He sounded suddenly angry. As if, by betraying Sharyn's trust, Kling had somehow betrayed *his* trust as well. Something was sounding a warning note. Kling almost backed off. He took a deep breath.

"She thinks I didn't trust her because . . ."

Brown turned from the wheel.

"Because she's black," Kling said.

"Well?" Brown said. "*Is* that the reason?"

"I don't think so."

"Then why does *she* think so?"

"That's what I'm asking you, Artie."

"What, exactly, *are* you asking me, Bert? Are you asking me would a black woman think her white partner who followed her was unconsciously harboring the thought that all blacks are devious and deceitful and not to be trusted?"

"Well, no, I . . ."

"I'm your partner, too, Bert. Do you think *I'm* devious, deceitful, and not to be trusted?"

"Come on, Artie."

"So what are you asking me, Bert?"

"I guess I'm asking . . . I don't know what I'm asking."

"I never dated a white woman in my life," Brown said.

Kling nodded.

"Only white men I really know are on the squad. I trust them like they were my own brothers."

Heat ballooned into the car. The traffic sounds were deafening.

"You're asking me will it work, isn't that it? You're asking me will black and white ever work? I'm telling you I don't know. I'm saying there's centuries here, Bert. Too damn many centuries. I'm telling you I hope so. I hope you find a way, Bert. There's more than just you and Sharyn here, man, you know what I'm saying? There's more."

He nodded, looked at Kling one more time, and then turned back to the road and the traffic ahead, hunkering over the wheel, still nodding.

Professor Duncan Knowles was wearing a purple butterfly bow tie patterned with little white daisies. He looked as if he might be ready to take off into the wind. Lavender button-down shirt to complement the tie. Tan linen suit. Sitting behind his corner-window desk, mid-morning sunshine setting the campus outside ablaze in golden green.

"A terrible thing," he told the detectives. "Terrible. What happened to Christine, of course, but also terrible for the department and for Baldwin itself."

Knowles was the head of Baldwin University's English Department. Kling hoped he wasn't equating Christine Langston's murder with the school's reputation. Brown was wondering where he'd bought the big bow tie. He was wondering how he'd look in a similar tie. Wondering if his wife, Caroline, would go for him in a tie like that one.

"A big-city campus," Knowles said, "you might expect unfortunate incidents such as this one . . ."

Unfortunate incidents, Kling thought.

"... but security here at Baldwin is unusually good. We've never had anything like this happen before. Never in our history. No one has ever wandered in from outside, intent on mischief."

"But someone did," Brown said. "Last night."

"Exactly my point," Knowles said. "This is terrible for the school. Well, look at these," he said, and slapped the palm of his hand onto the morning newspapers spread over his desk-top. "Christine was murdered last night, and already the newspapers are in a feeding frenzy. Look at this headline. 'Are Our Campuses Safe?' A single incident..."

Incident, Kling thought.

"... and they're making it sound like an epidemic."

"What we're trying to do," Brown said, "is find some link between Christine's murder and two other cases we're investi..."

"Oh, yes, and don't think the papers aren't making hay of *that* as well. 'The Glock Killer'! Making him sound like Jack the Ripper. Three murders coincidentally..."

"We don't think they're coincidences," Brown said.

"There must be thousands of such weapons in this city..."

"No, the same gun was used in each of the murders."

"Well, that's beyond me," Knowles said, and spread his arms like wings, enforcing the notion that his huge bow tie might indeed be a propeller. Brown still wondered where he'd bought it.

"We have the other victims' names," Kling said, and reached into his inside jacket pocket for his notebook. "It's unlikely any of them were students of hers at any time..."

"Why do you say that?"

"Well . . . their ages, for one thing." He had opened the notebook now, and was consulting it. "Or did she teach any adult night classes?"

"No. Well, she taught one class at night, yes. But that was a seminar. And these were young students as well. She taught three day classes a week, you see, two hours for each class. One on Modern Poetry, and two on the Romantic Poets. Those would have been Keats, Shelley, Wordsworth, and Byron. The course was divided into two sections."

"So altogether she taught six hours a week."

"Well, plus the seminar, of course. That would have been another two hours a week. Eight hours in all."

"And she taught this seminar at night?"

"Yes. Thursday nights, from seven to nine P.M. On 'Keats and the Italian Influence.' Either in her classroom or her office. There were only half a dozen students in the class . . . seven or eight at the most. Certainly no more than that."

"But this would've been a *Thursday* night, you say."

"Yes."

"Why would she have been on campus on a *Wednesday* night?"

"Any number of reasons. She may have been preparing lesson plans, or grading papers . . . or doing research in the library. The library closes at nine."

"What sort of research?"

"I know she was writing a paper for the PMLA. About the influence Charles Lamb's sister had on his work."

PMLA? Kling wondered. Pre-Menstrual something or other?

"She was quite ill, you know, his sister, Mary. In fact, in a fit of temporary insanity, she killed their mother."

Brown raised his eyebrows.

So did Kling.

"Oh yes," Knowles said. "Lamb had to place her in a private mental institution. Well, he was not without his own mental problems, you know. After a disastrous love affair, he himself had a breakdown. Spent a great deal of time in an asylum in Hoxton, yes."

"And Professor Langston was writing a paper on this?"

"Yes, hoping to have it published in one of the Modern Language Association's journals. On how Lamb's sister affected his work, yes. She titled it 'The Madness of Mary Lamb.' We joked about that a lot."

"Joked about it?" Brown said.

"Oh yes."

"Who did?"

"Her colleagues in the department. We called it 'Mary Had a Little Madness.'"

"So you think she might've spent some time in the library the night she was killed," Kling said.

"Possibly, yes. I'm sure you can check that."

"But normally, what time would her classes have ended?"

"Well, except for the seminar . . ."

'On Thursdays . . ."

"Yes. Except for that, she taught afternoon classes. Three to five."

"All young people."

"Yes."

"Does the name Alicia Hendricks mean anything to you?"

"No, I'm sorry."

"One of the victims. Fifty-five years old," Kling said. "How about Max Sobolov, fifty-eight? Blind?"

"No. Neither of them. And, as you say, they couldn't have been Christine's students here at Baldwin. Far too old."

"Any other way she might have been connected to them?"

"I'm not sure what you mean."

"Well," Brown said, "is it possible they were *relatives* of one of her students? Or *friends*? Or in any other way linked to Professor Langston?"

"How would I know that?"

"Can we check your records?" Kling asked. "Get the names of her students for the past several years? See if we come up with a match for either of them? Hendricks? Sobolov?"

"She taught here for the past twelve years," Knowles said. "She was a tenured professor. Surely you don't expect to go through all the . . ."

"Grudges sometimes go back a long time," Brown said.

"Grudges?"

"A student she failed? A student she embarrassed? The kid might've told a parent or a friend, might've initiated a grudge that . . ."

"I see," Knowles said.

He was thinking.

They both saw him thinking.

"Yes?" Kling said.

"I can recall only one such incident," Knowles said. "But the student's name isn't anything like those you mentioned."

"That only eliminates a relative," Brown said.

"What was the incident?"

"Christine threatened to fail this girl. The girl went over her head, came to me. I protected Christine in every way possible, but . . . you know . . . we don't fail students here. We simply don't."

"Would you remember who the girl was?" Kling asked.

Brown was still annoyed with himself for not having asked Knowles where he'd bought his fancy bow tie.

"You can get them anywhere," Kling said.

"Yeah? Where? I never saw a tie like that one before."

"Besides, you'd look lousy in a tie like that," Kling said.

"I think I'd look real cool in a tie like that."

"Too big for a big man like you."

They were walking across campus toward a building where a girl named Marcia Finch was attending a third-period class in Survey of Early American Literature. Marcia was the girl Professor Langston had threatened to flunk last semester.

"Are you suggesting I'm overweight?" Brown asked.

"No. Just large."

"Like Ollie Weeks?"

"No, he's obese."

"Besides, it's only large men who can entertain wearing big ties like that one."

"Entertain, huh?"

"I think Caroline might like me in a tie like that one."

"So go to the Internet, click on bow ties. You'll find all sorts of silly ties like that one."

"Nice big tie like that one," Brown said, nodding, visualizing himself in one.

"What room did Knowles say?" Kling asked.

They were waiting in the corridor outside room 307 when Marcia Finch came striding out, books clutched to her chest. Professor Knowles had told them they couldn't miss her . . .

"She's an assertive little girl, blonde, quite confident of her own good looks. She exudes . . . shall we say . . . a certain aura of self-assurance?"

. . . and they spotted her at once now. Twenty-one, twenty-two years old, a senior here at Baldwin, wearing a short blue pleated skirt, a blue sweatshirt lettered with the words BALDWIN U in white, and flat leather sandals to match the blue of the skirt and shirt. She laughed at something a girl companion said, waggled the fingers of her left hand in farewell, and turned to see a big blond guy and a big black guy standing in her path.

"Ex*cuse* me?" she said, making it sound like, "Get the fuck out of my way, okay?" and was starting to step around them, when Brown said, "Miss Finch?"

"Yes?"

He flashed the tin.

"Detective Brown," he said. "My partner, Detective Kling. Few questions we'd like to ask you."

"My father's a lawyer," she said at once.

"You won't need a lawyer, miss," Brown said. "Let's find a place we can sit and chat, shall we?"

"What about?"

"Little fracas you had with Professor Langston last semester."

"I think I'll call my father," Marcia said.

"Miss," Kling said, "let's make this easy, okay?"

She turned to look at him. Maybe it was the hazel eyes. Maybe it was the calm in his voice. Maybe she was a racist who preferred dealing with Mr. Blond WASP here. Whatever it was, she nodded briefly and led them outside.

They sat in golden sunshine on a bench outside Coswell Hall. Marcia on the right, Kling in the middle, Brown on the far left, both detectives turned to face her. Marcia sat with her legs crossed, books sitting on the path beside the bench, addressing herself entirely to Kling, telling her story to Kling alone. Sitting there, Brown could have been made of stone the color of his name.

"The issue seemed to be attendance," she said.

"Seemed to be?" Brown said.

She ignored him.

"Professor Langston said I'd cut too many classes. She said I couldn't possibly have a grasp of the subject matter if I never attended any lectures. Have you ever been to one of her lectures?" she asked Kling. "Bore-*ing*," she said, and patted her mouth in a simulated yawn. "The subject matter in question—actually, I'd only missed one or two classes—happened to be Wordsworth. Section II was all Wordsworth. I argued that Wordsworth was perhaps the most tedious poet in the entire nineteenth century. Have you ever read *Tintern Abbey*? Or *My Heart Leaps Up*? Or even *Intimations of Immortality*, which is supposed to be a masterpiece?"

Brown hadn't read any of them.

Besides, she was addressing Kling.

"Are you familiar with any of these?" she asked him.

"I'm sorry, no."

"Well, take my word for it," she said. "In any case, I read all the assigned poems at home and felt well-acquainted with all of them. I saw no need to attend all of the scheduled lectures . . ."

"How many lectures were there altogether?" Brown asked.

"A semester is fourteen weeks long," she told Kling. "She spent two weeks on introduction and orientation, two weeks each on Shelley, Byron, and Keats, that was Section I. Section II was a full six weeks of Wordsworth, because she felt he was so damn important, don't you know?"

"How many of those six weeks did you miss?" Brown asked.

She looked past Kling.

Fastened an eye lock on Brown.

"I told you. One or two classes."

"Which was it? One or two?"

"Maybe three altogether. And maybe I was late for one class."

"So you missed at least half of them?"

"Yes."

"Cut half of your classes."

"Well . . . yes."

"And this was why Professor Langston threatened to fail you?"

"I knew the work. I told you, I did it at home." She cut off the conversation with Brown, looked directly into Kling's eyes. "Am I going to need my father here?" she asked.

"No, I don't think so," Kling said gently. "So what happened? After she said she was going to flunk you."

"I went to see Professor Knowles."

"And?"

"He said he'd talk to her."

"And did he?"

"Yes. I'm a straight-A student here. I've never had a grade below B in all my life!" She turned slightly, so that her knees were just touching Kling's. "Can you imagine what an F would have done to my average?" she asked, blue eyes wide.

Kling moved his own knees away.

Marcia tugged at her skirt, as if she'd been molested.

"So what happened after Knowles spoke to her?" he asked.

"Well, she just remained adamant. She told him the syllabus called for grading to be based on attendance, participation, and final exam. She told him it was outrageous to ask that she pass a student who'd cut half of her precious lectures. Even though I'd mastered the material at home, mind you . . ."

"I think it *was* outrageous," Brown said.

"Yes, well no one asked your opinion, did we?" Marcia snapped.

"Maybe you ought to call your father," Brown suggested.

Kling recognized him falling into a Good Cop/Bad Cop routine. He didn't think that was necessary here. Not yet, anyway. He snapped him an Eye Warn. Brown caught it, seemed to cool it.

"So what happened?" Kling asked.

"My father went to see her."

"Good old dad," Brown said, and Kling snapped him another look.

"Reminded her that I was a straight-A student, further reminded her that he was paying close to thirty thousand dollars a year for the privilege of my attendance at this institute of higher learning, and lastly reminded her that his law firm had contributed a hundred thousand dollars toward the founding of an English Department chair here at Baldwin U. I think she got the message."

"She passed you," Kling said.

"She gave me an A."

"And was that the end of it?" Brown asked.

She looked at Kling when she answered.

"That was the end of it," she said. "Look, I got my A, why would I even care about her any longer?"

They tended to agree with her.

"You're not a drug dealer by any chance, are you?" Reggie asked.

"What makes you think so?" Charles said.

"Well . . . all this," she said, and waved her arm to include the seventy-five-foot sailing yacht, and the champagne in coolers, and the iced caviar, and the uniformed crew, and the filet mignon the chef was preparing for lunch, and . . . well . . . generally . . . all this luxury. Because out there in Denver, Colorado, where Regina Marshall was born and raised, you didn't have this kind of money to throw around unless you owned an oil well or two, or were dealing drugs for the Crips or the Bloods.

"No," Charles said, smiling. "I am not a drug dealer." Though he could imagine her thinking so.

"In fact, the only time I ever went near drugs was in the Army," he said. "And that was marijuana. We all did marijuana in Nam."

The boat was under full sail, rounding the point of one of the small islands that comprised the Sands Spit chain. Sunlight danced on the water. Reggie and Charles were sitting under the blue bimini, sipping champagne. It was a little past noon. They'd been out on the water since ten thirty.

"Me, too," she said. "Just a little bammy now and then."

He wondered if she was asking him for marijuana now.

"Gee," he said, "I'm sorry. I didn't think to get any."

"I prefer this," she said, and smiled, and held up the long-stemmed champagne glass. She was wearing white jeans, a striped cotton tank top, and white sneakers. She looked like she'd been born on a yacht, though she'd told him earlier she'd never been on one in her life. This was his first time, too. Lots of firsts with Reggie. Lots of lasts, too, he realized.

"Sir, excuse me, sir."

The steward, or whatever he was called. Blond guy wearing a white uniform. Charles looked up at him.

"Sir, what time did you wish us to serve lunch?"

"I was thinking about one. Reggie?"

"One would be lovely," she said.

"Then would you care to see the wine list now?"

"Please," he said.

Reggie glanced at him approvingly.

"You know," she said, "I really do enjoy being with you, Charles. Are we going to do this always?"

"Sail around the city this way, you mean?"

"No, I mean live this way." She held up the champagne glass again, gave it a little appreciative nod. "Just live the hell out of life this way."

"As long as we can," he said.

"Aren't you afraid the money might run out?"

"Nope."

"Got that much of it, huh?"

"Enough to last."

"Just take me along, okay, Charles?" she said, and reached over to kiss him. "Just take me along."

You dig, you find.

In any murder investigation, the vic is treated somewhat like a perp himself. Any criminal record here? Any outstanding warrants? Anything in the distant or recent past that might have predicted violence in the present? You do your routine checks, and sometimes you get lucky.

That Thursday afternoon, Christine Langston's name popped up on a complaint filed in the Two-Six Precinct where she'd apparently been living at the time; this would have been some ten years ago, before she'd met Mortimer Shea. Professor Langston herself, then fifty-eight years old, had filed the complaint. This is what she told a detective named Joshua Sloate:

One January night at a little past nine, she was leaving the building at Harleigh Junior College, where she was teaching English at the time. She hailed a yellow cab just outside the front door, and gave the driver her address downtown near the financial district. At ten o'clock sharp, she dialed 911 to report an attempted rape. This was five minutes after she'd awakened to find the driver of the cab in bed with her, on top of her. She'd screamed, and he'd fled. She was now reporting the attempted rape to the police.

A video surveillance camera in the lobby of her building had captured an image of the assailant following her into the building at 9:45 P.M. He was described in the report as an Indian man in his late twenties, five-foot-eight to five-foot-nine, and weighing approximately 160 pounds. There were no signs of forced entry into either the building or Christine Langston's apartment. The complaint was subsequently dismissed as "unsubstantiated."

Kling and Brown wanted to know how come.

They found Balamani Kumar as he was walking out of the Townline Taxi dispatcher's office on Westlake Street. He was just coming off the afternoon shift. A thin, shambling man in his late thirties, he did not at all resemble what his given name meant in India; there was nothing of the "young jewel" about him. He seemed only a tired and defeated stranger in a strange land, battered and beaten by the big city.

"Mr. Kumar?" Brown said.

He stopped, seemed distracted for a moment.

"Yes?" he asked. Expecting trouble. Knowing that in this city, for a foreigner, for a foreigner of his color and background, there would always be trouble. Kling showed him his shield, not at all sure this would have a soothing effect.

"Yes?" Kumar said again.

"Few questions, no problem," Kling said.

He could tell Kumar didn't believe him.

"Let's sit down and talk, okay?" Brown said.

They walked to a coffee shop a few blocks away. They bought him a cappuccino. They sat outside at round metal tables in the fading evening light. They did not tell him that Christine Langston had been murdered last night. They did not know whether he'd heard about this from the newspapers or television. They merely wanted to know about the complaint she'd filed ten years ago. And why it had been dismissed.

"Because it was fabricated," Kumar said.

His speech was clipped, more precise than singsong, undeniably Indian in origin. His native tongue might have been Hindi, Marathi, Kannada, Tamil, Gujarati, Telugu, Bengali, Gurmukhi, Oriya, or Malayalam. Here, in the land of the free and the home of the brave, he merely sounded like a foreigner.

"In what way, fabricated?" Brown asked.

"Invented," Kumar said. "A lie. All of it a lie."

"Tell us what happened," Kling said.

What happened was . . .

She was coming out of the school, just approaching the sidewalk, where the large globes are at the entrance there on South Jackson, do you know the location? There. A well-dressed woman in her late fifties, I would say. Carrying a briefcase. She gave me an address downtown, near the financial district.

We began talking on the way downtown. She'd been to

India only once, she told me, long ago, when she was a young girl. On an exchange program. For the summer. In the Rajahstan. I myself am from the south. I told her I was unfamiliar with that part of the country, it is a big country, my country. Well, a continent. She told me she'd had an exciting time there. She told me India was an exciting country. She used that word several times. Exciting.

Before she got out of the cab, she asked if I would like to come up for a drink. She said she would leave the lobby door unlocked. She said she would be waiting for me. Apartment 401, she said. She would leave the door unlocked. She would be in bed, she said. Waiting for me. Please hurry, she said. I'll be waiting.

The streets down there are empty at that time of night. There are hardly any apartment buildings. Everything is closed that time of night. The offices, the shops, the restaurants. Everything closed. It was very cold in the streets. Empty and cold. I parked the taxi, and locked it, and went to her building. The lobby door was unlocked, as she'd promised. I took the elevator up to the fourth floor. The door to apartment 401 was unlocked. As she'd promised.

The apartment was dark.

I could hear her breathing in the dark.

I found her in bed. I took off my clothes and got into bed beside her.

When I climbed on top of her, she began screaming.

I ran.

I grabbed my clothes and ran.

I dressed in the elevator.

The policemen came to get me two hours later.

"It was consensual," Kumar said now, scooping foam out of his coffee cup, licking the foam off his finger. "The detectives realized that. She invited me. I don't know why she changed her mind. This was an old woman! Who would want to rape an old woman?"

You'd be surprised, Kling thought.

And wondered if that was why the case had been filed away as "unsubstantiated." Because who would want to rape an old woman, right? A woman in her fifties? Easier to believe she'd invited the cabbie upstairs, and then changed her mind, and phoned the cops to boot.

But had she?

Or had Kumar, in fact, tried to rape her?

Had this been a matter of an elderly lady kicking up her skirts for one last fling, or a lonely young man tasting alien wine, however aged in the cask?

Had Christine Langston been reaching back to her lost youth and the exciting days she'd known as an exchange student in India? Or had Balamani Kumar been clutching at any kind offer in an inhospitable land? Fifty years old? Sixty? Who cared? A warm bed on a cold January night. In his own apartment, he slept with five other refugees like himself, three of them on the floor.

Who knew?

Who would *ever* know whether the lady had invited him into her bed—or been violated there?

And, really, who cared anymore?

The lady was dead, and the skinny young Indian was still driving a taxi.

One thing they felt certain of.

There was no resentment here.

No hidden grudge.

No old scores to settle.

Balamani Kumar was not the man who'd pumped two nine-millimeter slugs into Christine Langston's head last night.

Or anyone else's head, for that matter.

The two priests sitting and drinking wine in the rectory of St. Ignatius Church could both remember celebrating Mass in Latin.

Father Joseph was seventy-six years old and already retired. Father Michael would be seventy-five in July. He had already advised his bishop that he planned retirement, but now he was having second thoughts. The Code of Canon Law set the age of retirement at seventy-five, but Father Michael still felt young and energetic, still felt he could lead his parishioners in celebrating Mass, hearing confessions, baptizing, ministering the sacrament, performing any and all things necessary to the advancement of the Church.

"How is it where you are, anyway?" he asked Father Joseph.

"Actually, the center's very nice," the other priest said.

"I mean, what do you *do* all day long?"

"Well, it's not like having an active ministry, that's for sure."

"That's exactly what I mean," Father Michael said.

"But it affords opportunity for contemplation and prayer . . ."

"I contemplate and pray now."

". . . without the rigors and demands of a priestly ministry.

And I'm quite comfortable, Michael, truly. The Priests' Pension Plan sees to my basic needs, Social Security gives me Medicare and additional income . . ."

"I'm not worried about any of that."

"It's you're worried about not being active."

"Yes. It's *retiring*, damn it!"

"You know, you could always consider merely lessening your administrative responsibilities. Take an assignment as a Senior Associate for a period of time . . ."

"Sounds delightful."

"Or just accept the path the good Lord has chosen for you," Father Joseph said, and made the sign of the cross, and finished his wine, and rose. "Michael," he said, "it was wonderful spending some time with you, but I must get back before they lock the doors on me and call the police."

The two men shook hands.

"Remember when we were at Our Lady of Grace together?" Father Michael asked, and led the other priest out into the walled garden. The roses were in full bloom, and the Oriental lilies spread their intoxicating scent on the balmy June night. They shook hands again at the gate, and Father Joseph walked off to the next corner, where he would catch a bus back to the retirement center.

Father Michael took a deep breath of the night air, and then closed and locked the gate behind him. As he was walking back to the rectory, he thought he heard a sound behind him.

Turning, he said, "Yes?"

"It's me, Father," a voice from the shadows said. "Carlie. Remember?"

6.

Reggie was in the bathtub singing when Charles got back to the hotel at eleven thirty that Thursday night.

"Everything go all right?" she asked.

"Yes, fine," he said. "You have a nice voice."

"Thanks," she said. "They're from my cabaret act."

He looked puzzled.

"The songs," she explained. "From when I came east two years ago. Seventeen and full of beans. Well, almost eighteen, I'll be twenty this September. I had a choice of three places. L.A., Vegas, or here. I figured I'd do best here. But this is one tough town, believe me. Even getting in a booking agent's door is a monumental task. I was playing little dives out on Sands Spit, ever been out *there* in January or February? I'm singing about fiddlers fleeing while all I've got is a piano player at an upright behind me, and when it was time to pay the bill there were only two or three people in the place.

"Finally, in one of these joints there was this stand-up comic, good-looking blonde girl in her thirties, had an act where she mostly trashed her ex-husband. We got to talking one night, and she told me the way she made ends meet was to moonlight with an escort agency, though sometimes she wondered which was the moonlighting and which was the act, the stand-up she did in these dives, or the girl who dressed up in flimsy lingerie and went wherever she was sent.

"Which by the way," Reggie said, "I haven't called the agency in more than a week now, they must be wondering what the hell happened to me. I told them I had my period, but how long can *that* last, am I right? I just hope they don't send one of their goons looking for me. Annie told me they have these goons, though I've never had the pleasure, thank you. Annie is the stand-up comic who first put me in contact with Sophisticates, that's the agency you called, remember?

"Anyway, Annie told me everything in life has its side effects. You do one thing, you take one road, it leads someplace, it has its side effects. What if I'd gone to L.A., and landed a good gig in a club on the Strip, and what if a movie director or an agent had spotted me there, I could be a movie star now, am I right? I could have a house in Palm Desert. Would you like to go to Palm Desert sometime? I would love that. You know, I still think of myself as a singer who's turning tricks on the side so I'll be *able* to sing. But maybe it's the other way around, maybe I'm just a hooker with a good voice, maybe the singing is just a side effect of the hooking, or is it vice versa?"

"You're not a hooker, Reg," he said.

"I like that. Reg. Only one who ever called me Reg was my kid brother, who couldn't pronounce Regina. Which name I hate, by the way. Do you like being called Charles? It sounds so formal. Have you always called yourself Charles?"

"Well, different names at different times of my life."

"What'd they call you in the Army?"

"Charlie. Though we also called the enemy that. Charlie. The Vietcong. They were Charlie to us."

"And other times? Before you went in the Army?"

"Chuck."

"I like that. Come dry my back, Chuck," she said, and stepped out of the tub.

"That was in junior high and high," he said, taking a towel from the rack, beginning to work on her back. "I should've kept it in the Army, huh? Differentiate me from the enemy."

"How come you didn't?"

"I dunno. In Basic, they just started calling me Charlie. So I accepted it. You accept lots of things in life."

"Side effects," she said.

"Yes. I suppose."

"What'd they call you when you were a kid?"

"Carlie."

"Get out," she said. "Definitely *not.*"

"My mother hung that on me."

"Is she still alive?"

"Yes."

He hesitated a moment, and then said, "She left when I was eight." Hesitated again. "I lost track of her."

"Left?"

"My father, the family. She abandoned us. Later married the guy she'd run off with, I didn't even know his name, my father never talked about it. I was just a kid, my brother and I were just kids when she left. I was still called Carlie then. They only started calling me Chuck in junior high."

"Do you still see your brother?"

"No, he died of cancer twelve years ago. Funny the way things turn out, isn't it? I was in a war zone, I came out alive. But cancer takes my brother when he's only forty-eight."

"Side effects," she said, and nodded. "Has anyone ever called you Chaz?"

"Chaz? No."

"May I call you Chaz?"

"Sure."

"Starting right now, okay? That's your new name. Chaz."

"Okay."

"Do you like it?"

"Yes, I think I do."

"What do we have planned for tomorrow, Chaz?"

"I thought I'd let you decide."

"Let's take the Jag out again. I really enjoyed that."

"Head upstate maybe."

"Yes. Maybe stay overnight at a little bed and breakfast . . ."

"Well, no, I can't do that. Not tomorrow night."

Her face fell.

"There's someone I have to see tomorrow night. But it'll be the last time, I promise. After that, I'm free."

"I thought maybe you didn't like my singing," she said.

"I love your singing."

"Shall I sing for you again?"

"I would love you to sing for me again."

So now, at close to midnight, she sat up in bed, the sheet below her waist, her cupcake breasts dusted with freckles, and she sang to him about Natchez to Saint Joe and moonlight and music and not knowing if you can find these things and about there was a strange enchanted boy and about it being quarter to three and no one in the place except you and me.

And when she finished singing, she cuddled in his arms again, and said, "I love you, Chaz."

And he said, "I love you, too, Reg."

"Well, well, well," Detective Oliver Wendell Weeks said. "Another dead priest."

This as if a dead priest showed up every day of the week. Last one he could remember, in fact, was the one over in the Eight-Seven, years ago, young priest snuffed while he was at vespers. This one was an old priest.

"Ancient, in fact," Detective Monoghan said.

"Got to be ninety-six in his bare feet," Detective Monroe said.

The two Homicide detectives were looking down at the body as though it were a wrapped mummy in one of the city's museums, instead of a fresh corpse here on the stone floor off the church's garden. The nun who'd found him was still trembling. She was no spring chicken herself. In her fifties, Ollie guessed, more or less. She'd told the responding patrolmen she'd been a nun for the past twenty years. Would've made her around thirty when she joined the church. Both Homicide detectives were wondering what she looked like with no clothes on. Ollie was wondering the same thing.

"Two in the face," Monroe said.

"Do dee M.O. strike a familiar note, Ruby Begonia?" Monoghan said.

"Six-to-five a Glock was the weapon."

Ollie didn't know what they were talking about.

"The Glock Murders," Monroe explained.

"The Geezer Murders," Monoghan said.

"All over the newspapers."

"Television, too."

"This makes what? Number Three?"

"Four," Monoghan said. "If it's the same Glock."

"Let me in on it, okay?" Ollie said.

He hated Homicide cops. Hated the dumb regulations in this city that made their appearance mandatory at the scene of any murder or suicide. Their role was quote advisory and supervisory unquote. Which meant they stood around with their thumbs up their asses, demanding copies of all the paperwork. Besides, both Monoghan and Monroe could stand going on diets. So could the two patrolmen who'd first responded. Not to mention the nun. When you were in love, the whole world could stand losing a little weight. Not that Ollie was in love.

"Guy's been running all over the city killing old farts," Monoghan said.

"With a Glock nine," Monroe said.

"Should be an easy one then," Ollie said, and turned to the first overweight uniform. "What's the nun's name?" he asked.

"Sister Margaret."

"How'd she come upon the priest?"

"Came out to see if the garden gate was latched."

"She live here, or just visiting?"

"Got a room over on the other side of the church."

Ollie nodded.

"You think the old priest was banging her?" Monroe asked his partner.

"Would *you* bang her?" Monoghan said.

"He'd bang anything that moves," Ollie said.

"Yeah, yeah," Monroe said, but the thought of having sex with a nun was stimulating in a primitive pagan sort of way. Monoghan found it vaguely exciting, too. So did Ollie, for that matter. The nun stood there trembling, saying her beads, poor soul. Ollie walked over to her.

"Sister Margaret," he said, "I want to tell you how sorry I am for your loss."

Actually, he didn't give a damn one way or the other, one priest more or less in this vale of tears, especially a guy had to be a hundred years old.

"But I have to ask a few questions, if you feel up to it," he said.

The nun nodded, whimpering into her beads.

"What time was it that you found the victim . . . by the way, what is his name?"

"Father Michael Hopwell," she said.

"I understand you came out here into the garden to lock the gate . . ."

"To *see* if it was locked."

"And was it?"

"I didn't check. I found Father Michael and ran right back inside."

"So if it's unlocked now, it would have been unlocked then," Ollie said.

"Or vice versa," Sister Margaret agreed, nodding.

One thing he couldn't stand was a smartass nun.

"You went inside . . ." he prompted.

"Yes, and immediately called the police."

"Knew he was dead, did you?"

"Knew he was hurt. All the blood . . ."

She shook her head.

"See anyone when you first came out here in the garden?"

"No. Actually, I'd hardly stepped outside when I saw him lying there. I turned right around, ran right back in again."

"Hear any shots before you came outside?"

"No."

"When's the last time you saw Father Michael alive?"

"When Father Joseph arrived. I took him back."

"Took who back?"

"Father Joseph."

"Back where?"

"To the rectory."

"And Father Joseph is?"

"An old friend of Father Michael's. He's retired now. He comes here often."

"What time did he get here tonight?"

"Around eight o'clock."

"And left when?"

"A little after ten."

"You saw him leave?"

"No, I heard them exchanging 'good nights.'"

"But you didn't hear any shots?" Ollie said, surprised.

"No. I went into the chapel to say complin before I went to bed."

"Complin?"

"That's the last prayer of the day."

"Didn't hear any shots all that time?"

"The chapel walls are thick."

"Tell me about this Father Joseph."

"They were priests together at Our Lady of Grace, in Riverhead."

"They get along?"

"Oh yes. Get along? Of course. They're old friends."

"Where is he now, this Father Joseph?"

"He lives in the community center on Stanley Street."

Ollie looked at his watch.

It was ten past midnight.

He wondered what time priests went to bed. Well, retired priests. He wondered who paid for a priest's retirement. He wondered who'd shot Father Michael here.

"Who's got these other Glock murders?" he asked Monroe.

"The Eight-Seven," Monroe said.

"Well, well, well," Ollie said.

In the middle of the night, he woke up screaming.

She sat up, yelled, "Chaz! What is it?"

"A nightmare," he said.

But he was doubled over in bed, clutching his abdomen.

He lay beside her, trembling. He felt cold to the touch. She held him close. In a little while, he got out of bed and went into the bathroom. She heard the water in the sink running. He was in there for five minutes before he came back to bed.

"Tell me the dream," she said.

He hesitated, thinking. Then he said, "It was in Nam."

He was still holding his belly. The chills seemed to be gone, though.

"This woman and her baby are sitting on the hood of a Jeep. We're supposed to transport them back to where an interpreter is waiting to question the woman. Well, the girl, actually; she's no more than nineteen. The sergeant thinks the girl is a spy for the Vietcong, I don't know what gave him that idea.

"The sergeant is driving the Jeep. He likes to drive. I'm riding shotgun. M-1 in my lap. The girl is sitting on the hood of the vehicle. Baby in one arm, holding the baby tight. Other arm extended, stiff, hand clutching this like sort of handle on the hood, so she won't fall off with her baby. The road is rutted and bumpy, these mud roads they had over there, between the rice paddies . . ."

He began trembling again.

"I don't remember the rest of it," he said.

When she got up to pee later, he was sound asleep.

She kept thinking about his dream. After she'd washed her hands, she opened the door to the medicine chest over the sink.

There were five bottles of prescription pain relievers in there.

She wondered if he'd had a nightmare at all.

It certainly had been very nice to fall into two gratuitous drug busts while investigating a pair of homicides. But these windfalls hadn't brought them any closer to learning who had killed the blind violinist, or the cosmetics sales rep, or even the university professor. Nor did it much endear them to Connors and Brancusi, the two Narcotics cops who now had Internal Affairs to deal with because some punk night-club manager was making noises about having greased them for protection. The things a desperate ex-con would say to avoid taking another fall!

And now, to make matters worse, a dead priest had turned up last night in the Eight-Eight.

And guess who'd caught the case?

"Now the usual thing that would happen here," Ollie explained to the assembled detectives of the Eight-Seven that Friday morning, "would be if a person caught a body that he later learned had been shot with the same pistol used in three previous murders another squad had been investigating—fruitlessly, I might add—since the sixteenth of the month . . ."

This was now the twenty-fifth day of June. The clock on the squadroom wall read 9:10 A.M.

"The *usual* thing that would happen would be for the responding detective to cite FMU, and then run the paper over posthaste to the squad that originally caught the squeal, in this case yours precisely, the Famous Eighty-seventh."

He paused to have his droll sarcasm appreciated.

"But it so happens that my plate at the moment is both literally and figuratively empty . . ."

He did not expect any of the cops here in this room to understand or appreciate such literary terms, but the fact was that there'd been a dearth of murders in his own precinct and besides he was on a diet, hence the empty plates all around . . .

". . . and so I've decided to join forces with you, so to speak, and take upon myself the investigation of the priest's murder, whose name happens to be Father Michael Hopwell, should this be of any interest to you. And also to lend whatever assistance I may deem myself capable of, ah yes, in the ongoing investigations of the Geezer Murders you are already pursuing."

The Eight-Seven detectives did not know whether this was a blessing or a curse.

"Thank you," Ollie said, "don't bother standing, no applause necessary," and executed a slight but difficult bow with one hand on his still quite ample middle, empty plate or not.

Ollie's idle comment notwithstanding, the tabloids spread on Carella's desktop that Thursday morning were still calling the string of homicides "the Glock Murders." Now that

Ollie was on the scene, would the murders be remembered from this day to the ending of the world as "the Geezer Murders"? Carella hoped not.

But look at the facts.

Four murders thus far, all committed with the same automatic pistol. Two of the vics in their fifties. One in her sixties. And now one in his seventies. These were not youngsters, Maude. These were people getting on in life, you might say. Given your average life span of what—seventy, seventy-five, eighty *tops*?—this put middle age somewhere between thirty-five and forty. Yes, kiddies, face it. You were rounding the bend at thirty, and middle-aged at thirty-five, imagine that. Fifty was fast approaching old age. Sixty was, in fact, old. Seventy was decrepit. Eighty was ready for the box. None of these victims had been skipping off to kindergarten with a lunch pail in one hand and a box of crayons in the other. In all truth, the ages of the victims made the case sort of boring. Like watching Woody Allen kissing a beautiful blonde in one of his movies. If someone's about to die soon, anyway, what was the sense of going to all the trouble of killing him? Or her?

Well, you couldn't say the two fifty-something-year-olds were exactly at death's door. In fact, Alicia Hendricks had been a damn good-looking woman, in excellent health—and sexually active when she was younger, don't forget. And whereas the wandering violinist had been blind, he was otherwise in pretty good shape and certainly not rushing out to buy himself a burial plot. But aside from those two, the others seemed unlikely candidates for termination. Ho hum, let nature take its course was what most citizens of this city were thinking as they turned the pages of their newspapers to sexier stuff like the killing and torture of Iraqi prisoners of war.

Not that the tabloids weren't doing their best to make the murders sound as sexy as possible. The first thing they did was suggest that the Glock Murders were in fact *serial* murders, and then they quoted various FBI profile statistics common to most serial murders.

Never mind that until the murder of the priest last night, there had been only three killings . . .

(A serial killer is someone who usually kills more than *five* people.)

Never mind that the *now*-four murders had been committed in the relatively short space of six days . . .

(A serial killer usually slays over a longer period of time, sometimes even months or years, allowing a so-called cooling-off period between each murder.)

Never mind that the victims here were a mixed bag: a blind musician, a cosmetics saleswoman cum dope dealer, a university professor, and now a priest.

(A serial killer's victims are usually of the same type—prostitutes, hitchhikers, postal employees, what have you, but always easily categorized.)

Never mind that all the victims here were shot in the face at close range with an automatic pistol.

(Most serial murders are committed by strangulation, suffocation, or stabbing.)

One of the tabloids suggested that the serial killer here was trying to obliterate his victims' faces, a supposition with which a PD profiler actually agreed. All of the tabloids agreed that the primary motive of a serial killer was sexual, whether or not any sex had actually taken place before or after the murder. They also agreed that most serial killers were white males between the ages of twenty and thirty, which description fit half the stockbrokers downtown.

The detectives looking at all these statistics saw only two converging characteristics that might have marked their man as a serial killer: his victim's ages and their race: they were all getting on in years, and they were all white.

It was Fat Ollie Weeks who came up with the notion that *three* of the murders might be simple smoke-screen murders.

"Maybe he was only after *one* of them," he said. "Let's say the priest last night, for example. Maybe the rest were just to throw us off the track. No connection at all between them."

"Among them," Willis corrected, though he had to admit Ollie might have a point here. Aware that Eileen Burke was watching him, waiting for his further response, he merely said, "In which case, which one?"

"Was he really after, you mean?"

"You kill four people, you're *really* after each and every one of them," Parker said.

"I'm inclined to agree," Byrnes said, surprising Parker. "A smoke screen isn't usually this prolonged. Too much danger here of us closing in."

"I don't see the danger yet," Eileen said. "We haven't found any connection, so maybe Ollie's right."

"In which case, which one was he really after?" Willis insisted. "Who was the *real* victim?"

"Far as I'm concerned," Byrnes said, "they're *all* real victims, and he was after each and every one of them. Stay on all of them," he advised. Or warned. "And *bring* me something!"

Parker caught up with Ollie on his way out of the squadroom, and asked how things were going with his little Latina dish.

"Or do you plan on marrying her?" he said. "Is that it, Ollie?"

"Well, no. I mean, the subject hasn't come up. We've only seen each other a few times, whattya mean *marry* her?"

"Is exactly what I'm saying. But if there are no wedding bells on the horizon, then when do you plan to make your move?"

"I don't know what move you mean."

"Ho-ho, he don't know what move I mean," Parker said to the air. "I mean getting in her pants, sir, is what I mean. When do you plan to attempt this?"

"I didn't make any plans for that," Ollie said.

"Then start now," Parker said. "When are you seeing her again?"

"Saturday night."

"Tomorrow night?"

"No, *next* Saturday night."

"No," Parker said.

"Whattya mean no? That's when I'm seeing her. July third, next Saturday night."

"Wrong," Parker said. "Saturday night is wrong, July

third, July *when*ever. She'll know what you're planning, she'll . . ."

"I ain't planning nothing."

"She'll *think* you're planning something. Saturday night? Of *course* you're planning something! She'll be on High Alert, she'll put up a Panty Block."

"A what?"

"These Latinas, they call themselves, they know all kinds of ways to cut off a man's dick and sell it to a cuchi frito joint. It's called a Panty Block. If she suspects for a single minute what you're planning . . ."

"But I'm not . . ."

". . . she'll throw up a Panty Block like you never saw in your life. Here's what you gotta do," Parker said. "If you wanna get in this girl's pants, you first gotta create an ambulance."

"A what?" Ollie said.

"An ambulance. In French, that means like a setting."

"I always thought an ambulance . . ."

"Yeah, I know, but the French are peculiar. To them, ambulance means lighting, music, mood, the whole *setting. Ambulance,* is what they call it. They know about such things, the French. Saturday night is out. *Any* Saturday night. What'd you plan to do that Saturday night?"

"I told her to come over around seven. I told her I'd cook dinner for her."

"Oh boy! High Alert at once! Panty Block, Panty Block!" Parker said, and threw up his hands in alarm. "You want my advice?"

"Well . . ."

"Call her, tell her you want to change it to brunch. Tell her to come over for a nice Sunday brunch. Eleven o'clock Sunday."

"That's the Fourth of July."

"Good, that's a good American holiday, these Latina girls like to think they're American. Tell her you'll make pancakes. Pancakes are very American, very innocent. Tell her to dress casual. Blue jeans, if she likes. Most of these Latina girls don't *wear* pants under their jeans, you're already halfway home."

"Well, I'm not sure I want to *trick* her that way . . ."

"*What* trick? You're creating a safe ambulance is all. Nice Sunday morning brunch, the Fourth of July, who could suspect Wee Willie is lurking in the bushes?"

"It ain't so wee."

"That's just an expression. No one's disparaging your package."

"Just so you know."

"Call her. Change it to brunch."

"You think?"

"Am I talking to the wall here?" Parker said. "*Call* her!"

Dr. Angelo Babbio was the head of the Visual Impairment Services Team at the Veterans Administration Medical Center. He told them that *before* the Iraq War began, a survey here at VAMC estimated that the number of legally blind veterans in America would increase by 37 percent, from 108,122 in 1995 to 147,864 in 2010.

"That was *before* we started getting the figures from Iraq," he said.

"Do your records go back to the Vietnam War?" Carella asked.

"They go back to World War I," Babbio said. "What's your interest in the visually impaired?"

"We're investigating the murder of a blinded vet."

"And you think he may have been treated here?"

"According to his brother, yes."

"When do you think this might have been?"

"Late sixties, early seventies."

"Long time ago," Babbio said.

He led them through corridors lined with silent men sitting in wheelchairs. Elderly men on oxygen. Young soldiers recently returned from the desert. A bird colonel still proudly wearing his uniform, sitting motionless in his chair, his head bandaged. Facing a window beyond which was a green lawn and a blue sky he could not see.

Max Sobolov's records were already on microfilm. He'd indeed been treated here for rehab. Nothing they could do about his eyes, he'd lost both those to a mortar explosion. But they could teach him about spatial layouts, and environmental constants, and features of walls and floors, and how to use echolocation. They could teach him how to carry out complex tasks, travel intricate routes, locate difficult objectives. They could teach him the use of the long cane. They could teach him independence.

"We have him discharged after five years," Babbio said. "According to this . . ." He tapped the file folder. ". . . he was a difficult patient."

"In what way?" Meyer asked.

"Bitter, uncooperative. Lots of them come back that way, you know. They go off all gung-ho, and suddenly they're home, and they're still young, but they've lost an arm or a leg, or half a face, or they're paralyzed, or blind—as was the case with Sobolov here—and it gives them an entirely different perspective. Sobolov was in a lot of pain. We had to medicate him quite heavily."

"Did he become drug dependent?" Carella asked.

"Well . . . who can say? We gave him a lot of morphine, let's put it that way."

"Was he an addict when he left here?" Carella insisted.

"There is nothing in his record to indicate he was morphine-addicted when he left VAMC," Babbio said.

The detectives did not appear convinced.

"Look," Babbio said, "we're lucky we were able to release him as a functioning member of society. Most of them never get back to what they once were."

Carella wondered how many wars it would take.

They tried to imagine what this Riverhead neighborhood must have looked like forty years ago.

The elevated-train stops on the Dover Plains Avenue line would have been the same. Cannon Hill Road, and then the stations named after the numbered streets, spaced some nine blocks apart. The end of the line would have signaled an expanse of vacant lots, and then the beginning of the first small town beyond the city itself. Today, those once-empty lots were crowded with low-rise apartment buildings and shops where city melted imperceptibly into suburb.

No longer were there trolley tracks under the elevated tracks, and the traffic was heavier now. Today, Dover Plains

Avenue was lined with bodegas where once there had been Italian groceries or Jewish delis. What had earlier been an ice cream parlor was now a cuchi frito joint. The pizzeria and the bowling alley were perhaps there long ago, but the language spoken in them now was Spanish.

Times had changed, and so had the neighborhood where Alicia Hendricks and her brother, Karl, had once lived. But still anchoring the hood, like pegs at the corners of a triangular tent, were Our Lady of Grace Church, the Roger Mercer Junior High School, and Warren G. Harding High.

Alicia and her brother had each attended both schools. Karl had gone on from Harding High to prison. Alicia had begun work at a restaurant named Rocco's. They did not expect the restaurant to be there today. But there it was, sitting on the corner of Laurelwood and Trent, a green and white awning spread over the sidewalk, tables outdoors a little early in the season, waiters in long white aprons bustling in and out of the place. ROCCO'S, the sign above the awning read.

"I'll be damned," Parker said.

The present owner was a man named Geoffrey Lucantonio. His father, now deceased, was the Rocco who'd owned the place when Alicia worked here all those years ago. Geoffrey was seventeen when Alicia took the job. He remembered her well.

"Sure. I used to fuck her," he said discreetly. "Then again, so did everyone else."

Apparently, Alicia's reputation had preceded her from Mercer Junior High. Well-developed at the age of twelve, she had first gained a following as the "vacuum cleaner" of the seventh grade, a sobriquet deriving from her ability to perform excellent oral sex, a trend that was catching on among pubescent girls as a means of avoiding vaginal penetration and therefore unwanted pregnancies. By the time she reached the ninth grade, she'd tipped to the fact that blowjobs were a form of male exploitation, and she moved on to sex that brought satisfaction to herself as well. It wasn't long before her phone number was scrawled in telephone booths and on men's room walls with the advisory "For a wild ride, call Alicia."

"They used to have these Friday night dances at Our Lady of Grace?" Geoffrey said. "The guys used to line up around the block, waiting to dance with her. Just to get close to her, you know? Those tits, you know?"

Parker could just imagine.

"And she fell right into my lap," Geoffrey said, rolling his eyes. "I mean, talk about letting the fox into the chicken coop."

Genero figured he'd got that backwards.

Parker was a little envious. Beautiful, uninhibited fifteen-year-old coming to work in your father's restaurant? His own father had never even owned a hot dog stand!

"How long did she work here, would you know?" he asked.

"Of course I know! Two years. Left when she was seventeen. Went to manicuring school to get a license. Never heard from her since." Geoffrey hesitated. "Best two years of my life," he said, and sighed longingly.

Parker almost sighed with him.

That Friday afternoon, as they sat at an outdoor table on the sidewalk of a place called Rimbaud's in a small town perched on a river upstate, eating ice cream sundaes and sipping thick black espressos, she said, out of the blue, "Chaz, from now on, I don't want to charge you."

He looked across the table at her.

And suddenly his eyes brimmed with tears.

She was so startled, she almost began crying herself.

"Chaz?" she said. "Chaz?" and reached across the table to take his hand. "What is it, honey? Please, what is it?"

He shook his head.

Tears spilling down his cheeks.

He took out a handkerchief, dabbed at his eyes.

"I wish I'd met you sooner," he said.

"Any sooner, you'd be a pedophile," she said, and smiled across the table at him, and kept holding his hand.

He began laughing through his tears.

"Are you doing this because it hasn't been working for us?" he asked.

"What do you mean?" she said. "It *has* been working."

"I meant . . . the sex."

"Oh, that'll be fine," she said airily, "don't worry about it. We just need more practice at it."

He nodded, said nothing.

"We've just met each other," she said, enforcing her point. "We have to keep at it, is all. Learn each other. We have plenty of time."

He still said nothing.

"The sex is nothing, I'm ready to wait forever for it to

work," she said. "You want to know why? Because you're not like anyone I've ever met. Some guys, in the middle of the night, they like to start complaining about their wives, you know? I know you haven't got a wife, I'm just trying to explain something. They do that because they suddenly feel guilty about being in bed with a whore. So they blame it on the wife. The wife does this, the wife doesn't do that, it's all the wife's fault.

"Other guys, they like to tell you how brainy they are, or how macho they are. Middle of the night. This is because they're paying to get laid, and they want you to realize they don't *have* to pay for it if they choose not to, they are really something quite special, and they want you to appreciate this. Some of them, if you don't appreciate how marvelous they are, they start smacking you around. Those are the ones who are so very marvelous that they may knock out a girl's teeth or break her arm or suddenly pull a gun or a knife on her. Those are the ones you get the hell out of there fast. Run out in your panties, run out bare-assed, just get *out* before this truly gets dangerous. You weigh a hundred and ten pounds, and the gorilla in bed with you weighs two-fifty, never mind the Marines coming to the rescue.

"I've never been to bed with anybody like you, Chaz," she said, and reached across the table, and took both his hands in her own again. "*Never.* You never try to show off, you never brag about yourself, you never tell me you have an IQ of three hundred and twelve, or biceps measuring eight inches around. You're just . . . so full of *life,* Chaz. Just so . . . nice . . . and . . . gentle . . . and . . . and . . .

"You always treat me like a lady, Chaz. Always. Well . . . that's because I'm a whore, right? I know that. Always treat a lady like a whore, and a whore like a lady, right?"

"You're not a whore, Reggie."

"You keep saying that, I'll start believing it."

"Believe it," he said.

"Chaz," she said, and paused, and looked across the table at him, and said, "do you trust me?"

"Completely."

"Then tell me what happened last night."

"I don't know what you mean. When last night?"

"Where'd you go, for example? What'd you do?"

"I had some business to take care of. I told you."

"Late at night? You didn't get back to the hotel till . . ."

"Yes, Reggie. Late at night."

"Please don't get angry with me. I'm only trying to . . ."

"I'm not getting angry."

"Was that really a nightmare you had, Chaz?"

"Yes."

"Because, the way you were clutching yourself . . ."

"It was a nightmare, Reg."

". . . you seemed to be in pain."

"It was a painful nightmare."

"You've got a lot of pain pills in the bathroom, Chaz."

The table went silent.

"Chaz? What are all those pills for?"

"I sometimes get headaches. Remembering Nam."

"Headaches in your belly?"

"Let it go, Reg."

"Don't get angry, please don't."

"I'm not angry."

"Where are you going *tonight,* Chaz? What business do you have to take care of *tonight*? That's stopping us from staying at a bed and breakfast up here?"

"Old business."

"You told me this would be the end of it . . ."

"It will."

"The end of *what,* Chaz?"

"All this old business."

"*What* old business? Chaz, if I'm not a whore, then *trust* me, okay? Let me help you with whatever . . ."

"I'm all right, Reggie. There's nothing you can do to help, believe me." He squeezed her hands. "Believe me."

She looked into his eyes.

"Believe me," he said again.

She wished she could.

She wished she didn't feel that something very terrible was going to happen very soon.

"Christine and I were both fresh out of college," Susan Hardigan told them. "Both of us very young, and very arrogant, and I fear not very attractive."

She was sitting in a wheelchair in fading sunlight, a fading woman herself, in her late sixties now, they guessed, frail in a blue nursing home robe and woolly blue slippers, her gray hair pulled to the back of her head in a tidy bun. They suspected she had never been a pretty woman, but age had not been kind to her, either. Her crackling mind came filtered through a quavering voice, and she sat wrinkled and shriveled, as if cowering from death itself.

They had found her name on a stack of letters in Christine Langston's desk, the most recent dated April 24, almost nine weeks ago. They had called ahead and asked if they might come talk to her, and an administrator at the Fairview Nursing Home had told them that would be fine if they made the visit a short one. The drive out to Sands Spit had taken a bit more than two hours. Now, at seven in the evening, they sat on a porch in a wide bay window, dusk falling swiftly around them.

"And you've kept your friendship all these years?" Kling asked. He sounded surprised. He was still young enough to believe that friendships fell into clearly defined periods of a person's life: Childhood, High School, College, Grown Up. He couldn't quite imagine a friendship that endured into a person's old age, perhaps even to his death. But here was Susan Hardigan, who had known Christine Langston when they were both young teachers at Warren G. Harding High School in Riverhead.

"Yes, all these years," she said. "Well, we don't *see* each other all that often, especially since I began having trouble with my legs. But we correspond regularly, and we talk to each other on the phone, yes. We're still very good friends."

It occurred to both detectives, almost simultaneously, that she did not yet know Christine Langston was dead. Brown glanced at Kling, found him turning to him at the same moment. So who would tell her? They both suddenly wished they hadn't driven all the way out here today.

"Miss Hardigan," Brown said, "there's something you should know."

His voice, his eyes transmitted the message before he said the words.

"Has something happened to her?" Susan asked at once. "Is that why you're here?"

"Ma'am," Brown said, "she was murdered."

"I dreamt it," she said. "The other night. I dreamt someone had stabbed her."

Brown told her what had actually happened. He told her they'd been talking to associates of hers, students she'd taught, trying to get a handle on the case. Susan listened intently. He didn't know quite how he should broach the matter of Christine Langston's . . . sexuality? This was an elderly woman sitting here in a wheelchair, a spinster woman who reminded him of his aunt Hattie in North Carolina, albeit white. How did you ask her if she knew her close friend had once phoned in a false rape charge back then when you and I were young, Maggie?

"Did you know of any trouble she'd reported to the police?" Kling said, gingerly picking up the ball.

"What sort of trouble?" Susan asked.

"Curried favors from a cab driver," Kling sort of mumbled.

Curried, Brown thought. Well, an Indian cab driver.

"A cab driver curried favors from her?"

"No," Kling said, and cleared his throat. "Miss *Langston* curried favors from *him*."

"Nonsense," Susan snapped. "What kind of favors?"

Kling cleared his throat again.

"Sexual favors," he said.

Brown wished he was dead.

"Are you talking about that trick she played one time?" Susan said. "Is that what you're referring to?"

"What trick would that be, ma'am?"

"Back at Harding? The young man who needed an A?"

"Tell us about it," Brown said.

"But he wasn't a cab driver. He was a student."

Plainly about to enjoy this, almost rubbing her hands together in anticipation, Susan shifted in her wheelchair, leaned forward as if to share a delicious secret, lowered her voice, and said, "This boy desperately needed an A in the course Christine was teaching. Basic Elements of Composition, whatever it was. This was high school, he was a graduating senior, eighteen years old. But he needed an A from her to pull up his average from a C to a B. He'd applied to a college, some dinky little school in Vermont, and acceptance was contingent on his maintaining a B average."

Susan grinned. Her teeth were bad, Brown noticed. She suddenly didn't remind him of Aunt Hattie at all.

"Well . . . this is really rich, I must tell you. As a joke, Christine told the boy . . ." She suddenly winked at the detectives. "I don't know if either of you are old enough to hear this."

"Try us," Brown said.

"She told him if he'd go to bed with her, she'd give him an A. Joking, of course."

"Of course," Brown said.

"But he took her up on it!"

"Who wouldn't?" Brown said.

"Can you imagine! She's joking with the boy, and he thinks she's truly *propositioning* him?"

"So she explained that she was just kidding, right?"

"Well, no," Susan said, chuckling. "He was eighteen, she was twenty-three, this was consensual. Nothing wrong with that."

"Nothing at all," Kling said. "What was this boy's name, would you remember?"

"She never said. Told me the story one night while we were having dinner together."

"You're saying she went to bed with him," Brown said.

"Isn't that *delicious*!" Susan said, and actually clapped her hands. She leaned closer, conspiratorially. Her voice lowered to a whisper. "But that wasn't the end of it."

Neither of them dared ask what the end of it was.

"She gave him a C, anyway!" Susan said gleefully.

The detectives said nothing for a moment.

"Was he accepted at that college in Vermont?" Brown asked at last.

"No! He got drafted into the Army!"

Brown nodded.

"Isn't that the supreme irony!" Susan said.

"You know something," Brown said in the car on the way back to the city. "There are people who are ugly when they're young, and they're still ugly when they're old. Nothing changes there. Ugly is ugly."

They were caught in inexplicable post-rush-hour traffic. Brown was driving. The car windows were open. An incessant buzz seemed to hang over everything.

"I'll tell you something else," he said. "If you're getting a picture here of a mean old lady, then ten to one she was a mean *young* lady, too. And probably a mean little brat. Nothing changes. Mean is mean. Susan Hardigan enjoyed telling that damn story. They must have been two prize bitches back then, her and her good friend Christine. Both of them ugly, both of them mean."

"Yep," Kling said.

They drove in silence for some time, pondering the vast mysteries of life.

"Got time for a drink?" Kling asked.

"Caroline's waiting," Brown said.

When Carella got home that night, he explained that the reason he was late was there'd been another murder, and the Loot had them running all around town again.

"In the Eight-Eight this time, an old priest, same Glock," he told Teddy. "Ollie Weeks caught it, lucky us."

How many does this make? Teddy signed.

"Four."

Is it some nutcase shooting people at random?

The word "nutcase" was difficult to sign.

At first, Carella read it as "Nazi."

"Oh, *nutcase,*" he said, after she'd repeated it three times. "Maybe."

But he didn't think so.

First thing Kling thought was, She's a hooker.

Sliding onto the stool next to his, She's a hooker. Or was

that racial profiling? Or had he been drinking too much? Or did he just miss Sharyn too much? When you're in love, the whole world's black. Sharyn's words. The girl smiled at him. Very black girl, very white smile. Short skirt, crossed her legs. Smooth black legs, bare, shiny. He almost put his hand on her knee. Reflexive action. Been with Sharyn too long a time now. Once you taste black, there's no going back. Sharyn's words, too.

"Dirty martini," the girl told the bartender.

"What's that?" Kling asked. "A dirty martini."

The girl turned to him. "You don't know whut a dirty martini is?" she said, and then, to the bartender, "He don't know whut a dirty martini is, Louis."

"Tell him what it is, Sade," the bartender said.

"Sadie Harris," the girl said, and held out her hand. Kling took it.

"Bert Kling," he said.

"Nice t'meet you, Bert. Way I make a dirty martini," she said, and again to the bartender, "Correct me if I'm wrong, Louis."

"You're the one taught *me* how to make 'em," Louis said, grinning.

"You take two shots of gin," Sadie said, "and you add three teaspoons of olive juice. No vermouth. Just the olive juice. Then you either shake it or stir it . . ."

"I prefer stirring it," Louis said, actually working on the drink now.

". . . over ice," Sadie said, "and you pour it in an up glass, and add an olive. I like a jalapeño olive in mine, as Louis well knows. Thank you, Louis," she said, and accepted the stemmed glass. "You want a little taste of this, Bert?" she asked. "Li'l sip of this?"

"Why not?" he said.

She held the glass for him, brought it to his mouth. He sipped.

"Nice," he said.

"Yummy," she said, and brought the glass to her own mouth. Thick lips, berry ripe with lipstick. Black hair in corn rows. Earrings dangling. Legs crossed, skirt high on her thighs, one foot jiggling a strappy sandal, half on, half off. Low-cut silk blouse unbuttoned three buttons down. No bra. Silk puckered. Nipple on one breast almost showing. Not quite.

"So what do you do, Bert?" she asked.

"I'm a cop," he said.

"Oh dear," Sadie said.

"How about you?"

"Be funny if I was a hooker, wouldn't it?" she said, and winked at Louis.

"What are you?" Kling asked.

"A librarian."

"I'll bet."

"I'll bet you're a cop, too."

"You'd win."

"What are you, Narcotics?"

"Nope."

"Street Crime?"

"Nope."

"Vice?"

"Nope."

"Cause if you was Vice, and I was a hooker, I'd have to be real careful here, you know whut I'm saying?"

"I guess you'd have to be careful, yes."

"Good thing I'm just a librarian."

"Uh-huh."

"And you're just a plain old cop."

"Just a plain old Detective/Third Grade."

"Whut precinct?"

"The Eight-Seven."

"You think he's really a cop, Louis?"

"Man says he's a cop, I got no reason to doubt his word."

"Let me see your badge," Sadie said.

Kling reached for his wallet, opened it to where his shield was pinned to the leather.

"Gee," Sadie said.

"Told you," Kling said, and closed the wallet and put it back in his pocket.

"Wanna see my library card?" Sadie asked.

"No, I believe you."

"So what do you think the chances are of a white blond cop meeting a gorgeous black librarian in a bar on the edge of the universe?"

"Pretty slim, I'd say."

"You agree, though, huh?"

Kling looked at her, puzzled.

"That I'm gorgeous," Sadie said.

"It crossed my mind, yes."

"So if I'm not a hooker, why am I sitting here flashing my stuff at you? What kind of librarian would behave like such a brazen hussy?"

"A brazen hussy, huh?" Kling said, and smiled.

"A brazen hussy, is exactly right. Jiggling her foot, letting her boobs spill all over the bar. Lord a'mercy, my daddy would throw a fit."

"I'll bet."

"Let me have another one of these li'l mothas, Louis."

He poured her another drink.

Sadie lifted the stemmed glass.

"Would you like another li'l taste of this, Bert?" she asked. "I'm assuming you're off duty, seeing as how it's a Friday night, and you're sitting here drinking and all. Another li'l sip, Bert? Another sweet li'l taste?"

She lifted the glass to his mouth again, tilted it.

He sipped.

"Yummy, ain't it?" she said, and raised one eyebrow like a movie star. "But getting back, Bert, if I *was* a hooker, I would have to tell you how much I charge and all that, you know whut I'm saying? And even then, before you could make a vice bust, I'd have to be naked and accepting actual cash, whatever it is these girls charge, a hundred for a blowjob, two hundred for the missionary, five for the whole night, whatever, around the world understood. Then again, you're off duty, Bert, isn't that right? My question is: When is an off-duty cop *not* a cop? And how would he like to make love to a gorgeous black librarian?"

Kling looked at her.

Louis was a discreet ten feet down the bar.

"Li'l taste, Bert?" Sadie said.

"I think . . ."

She took his hand, placed it on her thigh.

Jiggling her foot.
Eyebrow raised.
He rose abruptly and went to the phone booth.

Sharyn answered on the third ring.

"Don't hang up," he said. "Please."

"I was in the shower," she said. "I'm soaking wet."

"Get a towel. I'll call you back."

"I *have* a towel."

"Sharyn, I love you to death."

Silence.

"Sharyn, let me come there. Please."

"No," she said, and hung up.

Sadie was still sitting at the bar. She ignored him when he sat down beside her. Then she took a long swallow of the martini, draining the glass, and placed it delicately on the bar top, and turned to him, her knees touching his.

"Mama give you permission?" she asked.

The old lady was walking her dog at almost eleven thirty P.M., not a particularly wise thing to do in this part of the city, but she did it every night at this time, and everyone in the neighborhood knew her, black or white, and she'd never had any trouble so far. When she heard the voice behind her, she was startled, but not frightened.

"Helen?"

She turned.

The dog didn't even growl, just stared into the darkness with her.

"Do I know you?" she asked.

"You should," he said, "it's Carlie," and shot her twice in the face.

As the dog turned to run, he shot her, too.

7.

He thought at first the girl in bed with him was Sharyn. Opening his eyes, first thing that registered was black. Then he realized her scent was different, her hairstyle was different, her face was different, this girl was not Sharyn Cooke. Oh, Jesus, he thought, and felt immediate guilt.

Almost ashamed to look at her.

But kept looking at her.

Black hair in corn rows. Ripe lips, free of lipstick now. Fast asleep, breathing lightly. Looked like a shiny angel. Earrings on the night table beside her. Clothes draped on a chair across the room. The clock on his side of the bed read 6:15 A.M. He was due in the squadroom at 7:45.

Was she a hooker?

In the bar last night . . . hadn't there been some talk about money?

He couldn't even remember which bar it was.

He kept looking at her.

She was quite beautiful.

She couldn't be a hooker, could she?

Her name was . . .

Sally?

Sophie?

Whatever her name was, whatever her occupation, she should not be here in his bed this morning. Was someone in Sharyn's bed this morning?

As if the bed were suddenly on fire, he got out of it fast, and virtually ran across the room to the bathroom. He closed and locked the door. He looked at himself in the mirror.

Maybe you didn't do anything but sleep together, he told himself.

Buy that one, and I have a good bridge I can sell you.

He kept looking at himself in the mirror. Then he got into the shower, and ran it very hot, and kept thinking over and again, What have I done, what have I done, what have I done?

She was sitting up in bed when he came back into the room, a towel around his waist.

"Hi," she said, and got out of bed immediately. "Gotta tinkle," she said, and rushed past him to the bathroom, long legs flashing, tight little ass, cute little boobs, the door closed behind her. He could hear her peeing inside there. He did not want this intimacy. This intimacy was reserved for Sharyn. But Sharyn wasn't here, *this* girl was here, *whatever* her name was.

He pulled on a pair of undershorts, trousers, threw on a shirt. Should he offer her coffee? Who *was* she, anyway? Had he paid her for last night? He hoped he hadn't paid her, he hoped she wasn't a hooker. He went to the dresser, picked up his wallet, thinking to check the bills there, see if he was now a hundred or so short.

The bathroom door opened.

She stood there naked, hands on her hips.

"Anything missing?" she asked.

Smile on her face.

"You still believe it, don't you?"

He said nothing.

"The fun I was having with you last night. In the bar."

He still said nothing.

"You still think I'm a hooker, don't you? My, my," she said. "Just how drunk were you, Bert?"

"Pretty drunk. I'm sorry. Forgive me if I . . ."

"Do you remember my name?"

"I'm sorry, no."

"Sadie," she said. "Sadie Harris."

He nodded.

"Librarian," she said.

He nodded again.

"Really," she said, "I'm a librarian. Last night didn't cost you a nickel. Go ahead, count your money."

"Well," he said, and put the wallet back on the dresser.

"How much of last night do you remember, by the way?"

He spread his hands helplessly.

"Well, *I* enjoyed it," she said. "Have you got a robe I can put on? Or are you going to kick me out without breakfast?"

He went to the closet, took a robe from its hanger, carried it to her, held it for her while she shrugged into it. His earlier guilt was changing to something else. He was beginning to feel rotten for the girl. If she really *was* a librarian, then . . .

"So where do you work?" he asked. "Which library?"

"Still don't believe me, huh?" she said, and walked familiarly to the cabinets over the sink, and opened one of them, and found a tin of ground coffee. "Chapel Road Branch, uptown near the old Orpheum Theater. I have to be in at nine, by the way. And I still have to go home to change into my librarian threads."

"I have to be in at seven forty-five."

"So we still have time," she said, and raised one eyebrow. "For breakfast," she added.

This time, he was cold sober.

This time, he was wide awake.

When she let his robe fall from her shoulders, he opened his arms wide to her and drew her close to him, and when she raised her face to his, he kissed her fiercely on the mouth. And then he lifted her off the floor and into his arms, and carried her to the bed.

"You still think I'm a hooker, don't you?" she said afterward. She was lying beside him, cradled in his arms. One hand was on his chest. Long slender fingers. Bright red painted fingernails.

"No," he said. "I don't think you're a hooker."

"Then why did I behave so sluttily last night in that bar?"

"Why?" he asked.

"Cause I liked what I saw," she said. "And librarians don't get out much."

"You seemed to know the bartender pretty well," he said.

"Louis. Yes, I do know him. I live right around the corner from there."

"Do you play that game often? Pretending to be a hooker?"

"Depends what I've been reading that week. Sometimes I pretend to be a rich Jewish girl from the suburbs."

"Are you really a librarian?"

"How many times I got to tell you, man? You want me to 'splain the Dewey Decimal System to you?"

"Is that another role?"

"The Dewey . . . ?"

"No, the li'l cornpone black girl."

"I can talk white, black, whatever suits you, dollink," she said, suddenly going Jewish. Then, for some reason, she reached up to touch his mouth. Her hand lingered there, her long fingers tracing his lips. "You have a beautiful mouth," she said. "I think I'm in love with you," she said. "Oh, pshaw," she said. "I got that expression from a British spy novel. Oh, pshaw. Man named Sykes keeps saying that to his assistant. 'Oh, pshaw, Shaw,' which is the assistant's name. Ask Louis. Two months ago I walked in talking British and being a spy. But I do believe I'm seriously in love with you," she said, and sat up, and leaned over him, and kissed him on the mouth. She pulled her own mouth away, looked him full in the face. "What's my name?" she asked.

"Sadie," he said.

"I've got a BA from Radmore U," she said. "I'm thirty years old. How old are you?"

"Thirty-three," he said.

"Well now, that's nigh on perfect, ain't it?" she said.

"Is that black?" he asked.

"That's white trash," she said. "Am I your first black girl?"

"No," he said.

"You're my first white man."

"Was I okay?"

"Oh my dear *boy*!" she said, and kissed him on the mouth again.

They both looked at the bedside clock again.

"I can't get enough of you," she said.

"Sadie . . ."

"Don't tell me you're married, or engaged, or even *dreaming* of having a relationship with anyone else," she said. "Because right now, you are going to make love to me again, and then we are going to discuss our future together, you unner'stan whut I'm sayin, white boy?"

"Sadie . . ."

"Now just *hush*," she said.

He hushed.

"We're beginning to get overwhelmed here," Byrnes said.

"I told you. The garbage can of the DD," Parker said.

"Where'd this one go down?" Hawes asked.

"The Three-Eight. In Majesta. Old lady and her dog."

"How old?" Carella asked.

"Seventy-three."

"He's upping ages," Meyer said.

"Softer targets."

"Same Glock?" Brown asked.

"Identical. Shot the dog for good measure."

"Killed him, too?"

"Her. A bitch."

"The dog, I mean."

"Right. A female."

"Where'd you get that?"

"From the Three-Eight's report. They sent us their paper soon as Ballistics confirmed."

"Sure," Parker said knowingly.

"What kind of dog was it?" Genero asked.

"We already went by the dog, Richard."

"I'm curious."

"A golden," Byrnes told him.

"That's a nice dog, a golden."

"Some people get very offended when dogs are killed," Hawes said. He was sitting by the windows, his red hair touched by sunlight, looking on fire. "You can kill all the cats in the world, they don't care. But kill a dog? They march on City Hall."

"Goldens?" Genero asked. "Or all dogs?"

"Point is we're overwhelmed here," Byrnes said. "Five homicides now . . ."

"Plus the dog, don't forget," Genero said.

"Fuck the dog," Parker said.

"Eileen, Hal? What are you guys working?"

"The liquor store holdups on Culver."

"Can you take on the dog lady?"

"Don't see how," Willis said. "We're sitting four stores alternately."

"Me and Andy'll take the dog lady," Genero said.

"We've already got the cosmetics lady," Parker reminded him.

"I like dogs," Genero explained.

"How're you doing with your professor?" Byrnes asked.

"Getting nowhere fast," Brown said.

"Where's Kling, anyway?" Byrnes said.

Brown shrugged.

Everyone looked up at the clock.

"So what do we do here?" Byrnes asked. "Cotton? You want to fly solo on this one?"

"Sure," he said. "Who caught it up the Three-Eight?"

"Guy named Anderson. We've got all his paper."

"I'll give him a call."

"Ask him what the dog's name was," Genero said.

According to Helen Reilly's neighbors, the dog's name was Pavarotti. A female. Go figure. Apparently, Helen was single when she was killed, but she'd been married twice before. This from several sources in her building, but primarily from her closest friend, a woman who lived across the street at 324 South Waverly. Hawes didn't get to her until almost three that Saturday afternoon.

Her name was Paula Wellington, and she was in her early fifties, he guessed, some twenty years younger than the dog lady. Good-looking woman with a thick head of white hair she wore loose around her face. Blue eyes. She told Hawes almost at once that three months ago she'd weighed two hundred pounds. Right now, she looked fit and trim.

"Helen and I used to walk a lot together," she said. "We were friends for a long time."

"How long would that have been?" Hawes asked.

"She moved into the neighborhood, must've been three years ago. She was a lovely woman."

"Where'd she live before this, would you know?"

"In Calm's Point. She was a recent widow when she moved here."

"Oh?" Hawes said.

"Yes. Her husband was killed in a drive-by shooting."

"Oh?" he said again.

"Gang stuff. He was coming home from work, just coming down to the street from the train station, when these teenagers drove by shooting at someone from another gang. Martin was unlucky enough to be in the wrong place at the right time."

"Would you know his last name?"

"It was a gang thing," Paula said.

"I'd like to check it, anyway."

"Martin Reilly. Well, *Reilly.* He was her husband, you understand."

"Of course," Hawes said, but he wrote down the name, anyway.

"They were very happily married, too. Unlike the first time around."

"When was that, would you know?"

"Had to've been at least fifty years ago. Her first marriage.

Two kids. She finally walked out after twelve years of misery."

"Walked out?"

"So long, it's been good to know you."

"Were they ever divorced?"

"Oh, I'm sure. Well, she remarried, right?"

"Right. What was her first husband's name, would you know?"

"No, I'm sorry. Luke Something?"

"Ever meet him?"

"No."

"He wouldn't have tried to contact her ever, would he?"

"I don't think so. No. I'm sure she would've told me. It was strictly good riddance to bad rubbish."

"The children? Would you know their names?"

"No, I'm sorry."

"Were they boys or girls?"

"I'm sorry, I don't know."

"Well, thank you, Ms. Wellington, I appreciate your time."

"You wouldn't care for a cup of tea, would you?" she said. "It's about that time of day, you know."

Hawes hesitated a moment.

Then he said, "I have to get back. Maybe some other time."

Paula nodded.

Fat Ollie Weeks did not like religion in general and priests in particular, but he hoped no one would write him letters on the subject because he simply would not answer them. He could not say he particularly disliked Father Joseph Santoro, except that the man appeared to be in his late seventies, and Ollie had no particular fondness for old people, either.

Why a man at such an advanced age hadn't yet tipped to the fact that wearing a long black dress and a gold necklace and cross might be considered somewhat effeminate was beyond Ollie. But he was not here to discuss sexual proclivities or the peculiar dress habits of the Catholic priesthood. He was here to learn what Father Joseph Santoro had seen or heard on the night Father Michael Hopwell was shot twice in the face, he being the last person to have seen his dead colleague alive, ah yes, except for the killer.

The retirement center at six P.M. that Saturday was just serving dinner to its fifty or so resident retired priests and nuns. Ollie knew these religious people had all taken vows of chastity and poverty, which he surmised included not eating too terribly much, or screwing around at all after hours, wherever it was they slept. Hence the somewhat gaunt and hungry appearance of many of the men and women seated around long wooden tables in the center's dining room. He was not expecting any kind of decent dinner, and was surprised to find the food both plentiful and quite delicious.

Sitting opposite Father Joseph, grateful that Patricia Gomez was not present to scold him about breaking his diet, Ollie dug into a roast beef cooked a little too well for his taste, string beans steamed to crispy perfection, and small roasted potatoes browned on the outside and flaky white on the inside. It was several moments before he remembered why he was here.

"So tell me what you and Father Michael talked about that night," he said.

"Mostly about his coming retirement," Father Joseph said.

He was eating like a bird, had to watch his girlish figure, Ollie supposed, the old faggoty fart.

"How'd he feel about that?" Ollie asked.

"Not too happy."

"Tell you about anything else that might be troubling him? Quarrels with his parishioners? Disputes within the church hierarchy? Anything that might have presaged his murder?"

Good word, Ollie thought, presaged. He doubted Father Joseph here had ever heard such a word in his life, presaged. The curse of being a literary man, ah yes.

"He was very well liked by everyone," Father Joseph said.

"How long have you known him?"

"We go back to our first ministry together."

"At St. Ignatius?"

"No. Our Lady of Grace. In Riverhead."

"When was that?"

"Fifty-some odd years ago."

"Everybody love him to death back then, too?"

Father Joseph looked at him.

"Do I detect a touch of sarcasm there?" he asked.

"None at all. Just repeating what you told me earlier."

"I never said he was loved to death."

"You said he was very well liked by everyone."

"Yes. But I did not say he was loved to death."

"Wasn't he?"

"There were naturally disagreements. There are disagreements in any ministry."

"Like about what? Molly wants an abortion, Father Michael says, 'Nay, that's against church law'?"

"Sometimes. Yes. Abortion can become an issue, even among the faithful."

"How about sex before marriage?"

"That can be another issue, yes."

"Or marrying outside the faith?"

"All issues that could possibly come up between a priest and his congregation, yes. That's why we're there, Detective Weeks. To offer guidance and direction."

"Think any of these issues might have come up during Father Michael's time in the priesthood?"

"I feel certain they would have."

"He mention any threats he may have received . . ."

"None."

". . . regarding one or another of these issues that may have come up . . ."

"No."

". . . at any time during his long priesthood?"

"Nothing. He was worried about retiring. He thought he'd have nothing to do once he retired."

"No more issues to deal with, right?"

Father Joseph said nothing.

"What time did you leave Father Michael the other night?" Ollie asked.

"It must've been around ten o'clock."

"To go where?"

"The bus stop on Powell and Moore. I catch the L-16 bus there. It's a limited-stop bus, gets me back here in half an hour."

"Hear anything while you were waiting for the bus? Any shots? Any loud voices? Anything like that?"

"Nothing."

"So you got back here at around ten thirty, is that right?"

"I didn't look at a clock."

"You said it was a half-hour ride . . ."

"Yes, but . . ."

"Or didn't you come directly here, Father Joseph?"

"I came directly here."

"So you must've got here around ten thirty, quarter to eleven, wouldn't you say?"

"Closer to eleven."

"When did you learn of Father Michael's death?"

"Later that night. Sister Margaret called to inform me."

"You don't think she could've shot him, do you?"

"Of *course* not!"

"Who do you think *might* have shot him, Father?"

"I have no idea."

"No one specific parishioner who might have disagreed violently with Father Michael's guidance or direction . . . ?"

"I know of no such . . ."

"Either at St. Ignatius . . ."

"No."

"Or before that? At Our Lady of Grace?"

"I can't think of anyone like that," Father Joseph said.

"Where's Our Lady of Grace, anyway?" Ollie asked. "Might be worth a visit, see if anybody up there has a longer memory than yours. Are you going to eat your dessert, Father? It's a sin to let food go to waste, you know."

According to Paula Wellington, her good friend Helen Reilly was a recent widow when she'd moved from Calm's Point, three years ago. Husband the innocent victim of a drive-by shooting. Biggest part of the city, Calm's Point. The area map showed two or three dozen precincts there—well, thirty-four, when Hawes actually counted them. By his modest estimate, at least that many drive-bys took place in Calm's Point every day of the week. Well, that was probably exaggeration. But trying to pinpoint a drive-by that had taken place more than three years ago . . . when there were thirty-four precincts to check . . .

Well, he supposed he could just run the name MARTIN REILLY through his computer, go back some five years or so, do a HOMICIDE check, he'd probably get lucky that way. But it would probably be easier and quicker, wouldn't it, to just talk to Ms. Paula Wellington again? Sure it would. So he called her at four that Friday afternoon, and asked if he might stop by, few questions that had come up, wondered if she could help him. She told him it was probably still tea time, anyway, so why not drop in, did he remember the address?

He remembered the address.

South Waverly Street downtown was packed with humanity when Hawes got there at a quarter to five. Kids in swimsuits running through the spray from open fire hydrants; this was now four days after the official start of summer. Men in tank-top undershirts playing checkers or chess on upturned orange crates. Dozens of women in cotton housedresses knitting on front stoops like so many Mesdames Defarges. White ice cream trucks trolling the streets like predators. Tweeny girls flashing long legs in short skirts, precipitate breasts in recklessly low-cut tops. Macho young men strutting their testosterone. And the cotton was high.

Hawes climbed past three women on Paula's front stoop. They gave him the once-over, figured him for a cop, and went back to their gossip. On the third floor, he knocked on the door to apartment 31. Paula called, "Just a sec," and then came to open it.

He wondered what the hell he was doing here.

She was wearing lime-colored bell-bottomed cotton pants and a white cotton tank top, no shoes. White hair pulled back into a ponytail fastened with a ribbon the color of the pants. Lipstick, no other makeup.

"You're early," she said. "Come on in."

"Sorry to break in on you this way."

"Hey, you gave warning," she said, and led him into the living room. It was decorated in what he guessed was Danish modern, all blond woods and nubby fabrics. A big mirror on the wall behind the couch made the room appear to be twice its size. "Did you really want tea?" she asked. "Or would you prefer a drink?"

"I'm still on duty," he said.

"So tea it is," she said, and went to where a kettle was already steaming on the stove. He watched as she prepared two cups. Outside, he could hear the street sounds of summer. She brought the tea and a tray of cookies to where he was sitting on the couch. In late afternoon sunlight, they sipped their tea and nibbled at their cookies.

"What I wanted to know," he said, putting down his cup, "when I was here earlier, you mentioned a drive-by shooting . . ."

"Yes."

"Said Helen Reilly's husband was killed coming down the steps from a train station . . ."

"Yes, the elevated station on Cooper and Duane."

"Cooper and Duane. That would make it the Nine-Seven Precinct."

"If you say so," Paula said, and smiled. "Is the tea all right?"

"Delicious," he said, and picked up his cup again.

"You said some questions had come up . . ."

"Yes. Well. Actually, that was the question. I wanted to know in which precinct the incident had occurred. The shooting. The murder, actually."

"Ah."

"Yes."

"So I guess it was easier to find out by coming here to ask me," Paula said. "Instead of going to the computer or whatever."

"Well, then I wouldn't have got the tea and cookies."

"I suppose not. Is that why you came here, Detective Hawes? For the tea and cookies?"

"No, I came here to ask if you'd like to have dinner with me tonight."

"I see."

"Would you?"

"Yes," she said.

Dutch Schneider was the Nine-Seven detective who'd caught the drive-by shooting three years ago. His precinct, and his squadroom, were in the shadow of the elevated structure that carried emerging subway trains from the city proper out here to Calm's Point. Every few minutes, a train would rumble past the open squadroom windows, reminding both detectives of the city's constant rattle and roar, causing Schneider to pause in his recitation and roll his eyes heavenward.

"At first, we thought Reilly *himself* was the target," he told Hawes. "Guy coming down the steps from the train platform, all at once a car zooms by, and *bango,* he's dead on the sidewalk? We figured the perp was somebody familiar with his habits, knew he was taking the train to the city that day, knew when he'd be coming back, was waiting to ambush him. Matter of fact, for a while we considered the wife herself a suspect. Thought maybe she'd hired somebody to ace the husband when he got off the train . . ."

"How'd that turn out?" Hawes asked.

"Loved him to death. Second marriage for her, the first was a lemon. Couldn't have been happier than she was with this guy, no reason at all to want him dead. We got off that kick right away."

"When did you figure it for a gang drive-by?"

"Not for a while, actually. I mean, this wasn't a bunch of street hoods sitting on a front stoop, flaunting their colors, rival gang drives by, opens fire. The shooting wasn't directed at anything but the steps coming down from the platform. And Reilly was the only vic. So we concentrated on the usual suspects for a long time."

"Who would they be?"

"Guys he used to work with . . . this was an old fart, you understand, seventy-eight years old, retired. Other guys he played poker with. Nobody had any reason to kill him. Then, out of the blue—"

Then, out of the blue, a train rattled by on the tracks outside the squadroom windows. Schneider rolled his eyes, tapped his fingers impatiently on the desktop. Hawes was suddenly grateful for the relative peace and quiet of his own turf.

"Where was I?" Schneider asked.

"Out of the blue," Hawes prompted.

"Out of the blue, this little Spanish girl comes up the squadroom, tells us somebody's gonna kill her boyfriend. Turns out this is right out of *West Side Story,* only it's two Puerto *Rican* gangs, not one white, one Spanish. But the same Romeo-Juliet plot, you understand? The girl's boyfriend is a member of the Royals and her brother is a member of the Hearts. Her brother warned her to break it off with him, she refused, so now they're gonna kill him. Well, who gives a shit? Why bother us with this gang shit? Figure it out for yourselves, okay? One less Royal on earth, gee what a pity. But, oh ho," Schneider said, and glanced toward the windows, as if expecting another interruption from the rapid-transit system.

"Oh ho," he said again, when he realized the coast was clear, "she *then* tells us that six months earlier, they tried to get her boyfriend when he was coming home from the city . . ."

"And this tied in with the Reilly shooting, right?"

"Same date, as it turned out, February twelfth, blood all over the snow. Her boyfriend was on the same train as Reilly, coming down the same steps as Reilly when he caught it. The boyfriend ran like hell cause he knew it was him they were after."

"Case closed."

"I wish," Schneider said. "Thirty-six guys in that gang, all of them with alibis a mile long. We hassled them from here to Sunday, but we couldn't break any of them. Whoever shot Reilly is still out there someplace."

"Bearing a grudge maybe?"

"How do you mean?"

"For being hassled?"

"This was three years ago. They're all either dead or in jail by now."

"You think one of them might have gone after Reilly's widow? Out of spite?"

"I'd put nothing past these jack-off gangs. But why would they bother going after an old lady? They're all into dealing drugs nowadays, these gangs. They got no time for settling petty grievances."

Drugs again. Two drug busts already in this case.

"Who's your gang guy up here?" he asked. "I'd like to talk to some of these kids."

Kids, they weren't.

Talkative, they weren't, either.

"Why should I talk to you?" Everado Rodriguez told Hawes. "I done something wrong in your precinck? I done something wrong in this city? What is it I done wrong, you mine tellin me, you come all the way out here to Calm's Point seekin me?"

"I want to know if the name Martin Reilly means anything to you," Hawes said.

"Oh, Jesus, *that* shit again?" Everado said. "The cops from the Nine-Seven were all over us about that, three years ago. We're back to that again?"

It was seven o'clock that Saturday night, and they were in the basement room the Hearts euphemistically called their "clubhouse." Everado was the so-called president of the so-called club. He was perhaps twenty-four years old, wearing blue jeans, a white T-shirt, and a blue bandanna Hawes assumed to be the gang's colors. There wasn't too much gang activity in the Eight-Seven these days; he wasn't quite sure how to deal with this twerp.

"You're clean on that one, right?" he said.

"Which one *ain't* I clean on?" Everado asked, and grinned, and turned for applause to one of his three henchmen lined around the room with their arms folded across their chests. They all grinned back. Hawes felt like smacking all of them across the mouth.

"There's an old lady who got shot twice in the face last night," he said. "Her name's Helen Reilly."

"So?" Everado said.

"Martin Reilly was her husband."

"So?"

"So the Nine-Seven gave you a rough time after Reilly was shot in a drive-by . . ."

"That's water under the bridge, man. We're all grown-ups now."

"Meaning?"

"Meaning my sister's married now, with two kids already. Why should I care about a crush she had on somebody from the Royals?"

"Maybe because it was your sister who went to the cops."

"She knows better now."

"Still pisses you off, though, doesn't it?"

"Nope. For what purpose should I still be angry? Everything's cool now, man. Why you comin aroun here, stirrin up trouble?"

"Know anybody named Alicia Hendricks?"

"No."

"Max Sobolov?"

"No."

"Christine Langston?"

"Who are all these people?"

"They wouldn't have come up here buying dope, would they?"

"Oh, we gonna talk dope now? This club is not involved in dope, no way, no how."

"I'll check with Narcotics, you know."

"So check. They're our best buddies, Narcotics," Everado said, and grinned at his henchmen again. They all grinned back. "You're on the wrong block, mister."

Hawes figured maybe he was.

She was wearing for their Saturday night out a simple black dress, white hair loose around her face, black high-heeled sandals. Her only piece of jewelry was a gold ring with a red stone, on the ring finger of her right hand, echoing the color of her lipstick. Hawes wondered if she'd ever been married. Beautiful woman, fifty-something years old, hadn't she ever been married? He also wondered fifty *what*?

"So where'd you get the white streak?" she asked.

She was drinking a Bombay martini on the rocks. He was drinking bourbon and soda. She was referring to the white streak in his otherwise red hair, just over the left temple.

"I was investigating a burglary, talking to the vic," he said, making it short; he'd only been asked a hundred times before. "The super rushed in with a knife, mistook me for the perp, cut me. The hair grew back white."

"Bores you, right?"

"Sort of. How old are you, Paula?"

"Wow! Right between the eyes! Fifty-one. Why? How old are you?"

"Thirty-four."

"Makes me old enough to be your mother. *Une femme d'un certain âge,* right?"

"Well, it's something we should talk about, I guess."

"I debated it, you know. For about thirty seconds."

"Me, too."

"There's enough trouble making a relationship work, we don't need the age thing."

"Exactly my reasoning."

"I just got out of a relationship that didn't work . . ."

"Me, too."

"So there's that, too."

"Catching each other on the rebound."

"Right."

"So what are we doing here?"

"I guess we want to be here."

"I know I do."

"Me, too. How old was this other woman? The one that just ended?"

"Late twenties? I never asked."

"Ah. But you asked me."

"Only because you're so beautiful."

"Nice save."

"How old was your guy?"

"Mid-fifties."

"More appropriate, right?"

"I guess. But somehow you don't seem inappropriate."

"Neither do you."

"So what shall we do here, Cotton?"

"Let's eat," Hawes said. "I'm starved, aren't you?"

So she ordered the roasted peppers with anchovies and mozzarella to start, and then the veal piccata as her main dish, and he ordered the bruschetta to start, and then the linguine puttanesca. He asked if she would like a white wine with her veal, but she said she really preferred red with *everything*, and so he ordered a bottle of their best Merlot. As the waiter uncorked it, and poured it, Paula said, "There's a genuine benefit to drinking red wine, you know. Other alcoholic products weaken the immune system and leave the body vulnerable. But they say red wine fights heart disease and cancer."

The waiter nodded in agreement, and padded off.

Hawes raised his glass.

"What shall we drink to, Paula?" he asked.

"I dunno," she said, and looked into her glass. "Depends on how *old* the wine is, don't you think?"

He caught her little quip, smiled, looked into his own glass, pondered a moment, and then nodded and looked across the table at her.

"Age cannot wither her," he said, "nor custom stale her infinite variety," and clinked his glass against hers.

"Lovely," she said. "But let's make a deal, okay?"

"Okay."

"Let's never talk about the difference in our ages again."

"Never is a long, long time."

"I hope so," she said.

They clinked glasses again, drank.

"Mmm," she said.

"Delicious," he said.

"How come you're quoting Shakespeare at me?" she asked.

"We just had a case where the perp was fond of doing that."

"The perp," she said, and nodded. "I guess I'll have to get used to cop talk, too."

"I guess," he said.

Over dessert, she told him that she'd been married for six years when her husband was called up from the National Guard to serve in the first Gulf War. He was killed in action a month after he arrived in Saudi Arabia. She'd been working at the time as an interior decorator, had since held a job at a house-and-garden-type magazine, and then in a department store's design section, and was now working for a small art gallery in downtown Isola. Hawes told her he'd never been married. He told her he'd been in the Navy during his particular war. He told her he liked police work most of the time. He promised he would not bore her with tales of the cases he was working, though at the moment . . .

And they both laughed when he started telling her about the four unrelated murder victims they were now investigating.

When their laughter ebbed, she said, "Cotton?"

"Yes?"

"I'm old enough to have been at Woodstock," she said.

"I thought we promised . . ."

"I'm making a different point. Back then, I ran around in beads and feathers, no bra. Back then, I went to bed with a lot of different guys. This was the sixties. That's what we did. Said hello and jumped right into bed."

He was listening.

"I'm not that impetuous nowadays," she said.

"Okay."

"What I'm saying is, we're not going to bed with each other tonight."

"Okay."

She sipped at her coffee.

He sipped at his.

"Are you angry?"

"Disappointed," he said.

"Me, too," she said.

8.

First thing Monday morning, right after the blues had mustered downstairs and filed out to their cars or their foot posts, Captain John Marshall Frick called Byrnes into his corner office, and read him the riot act.

"I just got a call from the Commish," he said. "He is not pleased. He is definitely not pleased."

Byrnes thought Frick should have retired long ago. He suspected that all the Captain did was sit at his computer all day long, e-mailing Old Fart jokes to other Old Fart captains in precincts all over the city. Not that Frick was truly old. What was he, after all? Sixty, sixty-five, in there? It was just that he was truly an old fart.

"Not pleased at all," he said, putting it yet another way. "He wants some immediate results on these Glock Murders. Immediate. He thinks we're fiddling around up here. He wants us to quit fiddling around up here."

"Fiddling around?" Byrnes said. "I've got the whole damn squad working twenty-four/seven, the whole damn squad's on overtime, he calls that *fiddling*? We're dealing with a case where maybe the motives go back *centuries,* you're telling me we're fiddling around?"

"I'm telling you what the Commish told *me.* He wants us to quit fiddling around and bring him some results. Immediate results. He's cut us enough slack, is what he said. He knows he owes us on the terrorist bust, but we can't ride on past glory forever, is what he said. We've got five vics so far, and Christ knows if this lunatic is done yet, and he wants results, immediate results, is all I can tell you! The papers and television are screaming!"

"You're the one who's screaming, John," Byrnes said softly.

"I don't like getting bawled out by the Commish."

"And I don't like getting bawled out by you," Byrnes said.

"Then stop fiddling around and bring me some *results*!"

At a quarter past nine that Monday morning, Hawes spoke to the young priest who'd arranged for Helen Reilly's funeral, and her burial yesterday. His name was Father Kevin Ryan.

"After the terrible tragedy three years ago," he said, and crossed himself, "there really were no surviving relatives."

"You mean the gang shooting," Hawes said.

"Well, what *appeared* to be a gang shooting, at any rate. One never knows the truth of such matters, does one? And they never apprehended the shooter, did they? Martin's sister discounts the gang theory entirely. She and Helen didn't get along, you know."

"Oh?"

"Or so some of the parishioners told me. In any event, she didn't come to Helen's funeral, so I guess there's some truth to it."

"Why didn't they get along?"

"I have no idea."

"What's her name?"

"Lucy Hamilton."

"Where does she live, would you happen to know?"

Martin Reilly's younger sister was seventy-four years old . . .

Everybody involved in this case already had one foot in the grave . . .

. . . and she still believed her late, unlamented sister-in-law had something to do with Martin's murder.

"I never for a minute believed this big *love* affair of theirs," she said, clasping her hands to her bosom in a mock swoon. "Tristan and Isolde, Eloise and Abelard, baloney. She was in an unhappy marriage she wanted to get out of, and my poor brother became her hapless victim."

Hawes knew when to shut up.

Lucy Hamilton was just gathering steam. A widow herself, she had no sympathy whatever for her brother's recent widow. Described her as a barmaid with no education and no manners . . .

". . . deliberately ensnared Martin, abandoned her husband and children the moment she saw greener pastures. I didn't like her the first time Martin brought her around, and I never *did* get to like her."

"Tell me more about these children," Hawes said.

"What?"

"You said she abandoned . . ."

"Oh. Well, that's what I deduced. Wouldn't you?"

"How do you know there were children?"

"My brother mentioned it one night. Married woman with a pair of kids. When he was telling me, for the thousandth time, how much Helen loved him. Said she'd adored him so much that she'd been willing to leave her husband and two kids for him."

"Boys or girls? These kids?"

"He just said 'kids.' I didn't press him, I didn't give a damn. When he met Helen, she was twenty-two years old, married, with two kids, and sleeping around with every man in sight. So Martin brings her home. And in the end, he gets shot coming down from a train station."

"You see these two events as linked, do you?"

"Don't you?"

"You think Helen somehow had something to do with your brother's murder?"

"That's what I told the detectives."

"What did you tell them, Mrs. Hamilton?"

"Told them she probably started sleeping around again. Told them my brother had become an inconvenience, just like her first husband."

"After almost fifty years of marriage, whatever? A seventy-year-old woman? Sleeping around?"

"A leopard doesn't change spots, Detective Hawes."

"Why do you say that?"

"I sensed it."

"You sensed that what they called their great love was really . . ."

"A sham," Lucy said, and nodded.

"I see," Hawes said.

"Which is why she got her most *recent* boyfriend to shoot my brother on the way home from the city."

"And this 'recent' boyfriend. Any idea who he might have been?"

"You don't advertise something like that."

"But we know she was living alone at the time of her murder."

"Appearances are sometimes deceptive."

"You think she might have been living with someone, is that it?"

"The boyfriend," Lucy said, and nodded again.

Hawes figured he was wasting his time here.

You can change your telephone number as often as you change your underwear. You can change your street address every fifty years or so, even more frequently if you happen to be upwardly or downwardly mobile. Every time you buy a new car, you can change your license plate number. And it's a simple matter to change your credit card numbers whenever you so desire. But if you live in the United States of America, there is one set of numbers that sticks with you for your entire life.

Nine digits across the face of a simple blue card.

Nine digits divided into three parts.

Area numbers, group numbers, and serial numbers.

The number assigned to you the first time you get a job, and the number that will stay with you forever.

Your Social Security number.

A call to Social Security Admin tracked Helen Reilly back to when she was Helen Purcell and further back to when she was still Helen Rogers and took her first job at the age of seventeen. Hawes knew that her first husband's name might have been Luke; Paula Wellington had suggested this. On the off chance that someone named Luke Purcell was still alive . . .

If so, he'd have to be in his late seventies or early eighties . . .

. . . Hawes checked all of the city's five telephone directories. He came up with hundreds of Purcells, but no Lukes.

A call to the Department of Records unearthed a death certificate for a Luke Randolph Purcell, who'd died of lung cancer seven years ago, at the age of seventy-one. Several phone calls later, Hawes recovered a marriage certificate from 1950, for a Luke Randolph Purcell and a Helen Rogers, and a subsequent certificate of divorce for the couple. But if Luke and Helen Purcell had had any children—boys or girls—before they went their separate ways, the kids were still largely anonymous in a city of largely anonymous people. Hawes called the office of Vital Statistics, and asked a man named Paul Endicott to see what he had on any children for a Luke and Helen Purcell.

"You know how many Purcells there are in the records down here?" Endicott asked.

Hawes confessed he did not.

"There are *thousands,*" Endicott said. "Purcell is a very common name. Would you yourself like to come down here personally, Detective, and go through the thousands of Purcells on file here? Looking for a Helen or a Luke to see what their fucking kids' names were?"

"I wish you'd help me," Hawes told him. "This is a homicide we're investigating."

By eleven o'clock that Monday morning, Hawes had gone through four of the city's five telephone directories and was working on the fifth, slogging through the book, dialing, and then identifying himself, and then doggedly asking the very same question of every Purcell who answered the phone: "Are you related to a Luke or a Helen Purcell?"

At times he felt like a telemarketer; people just hung up on him, even after he told them he was a detective. Other times, he felt hopelessly old-fashioned. In this day and age of instant messaging, there had to be a quicker, simpler way of zeroing in on the progeny of Helen and Luke—if, in fact, they even existed; so far, he had only the word of Helen's sister-in-law for that.

He looked up at the wall clock. Sighed. Ran his finger down the page to the next Purcell in the Riverhead directory. Jennifer Purcell. Began dialing again. Listened to the phone ringing on the other end.

"Hello?"

A woman's voice.

"Hello, this is Detective Hawes of the Eighty-seventh Squad. I'm trying to reach Jennifer Purcell . . ."

"Yes, this is Jennifer?" the woman said. Youngish voice, late twenties, early thirties, clearly puzzled. "What's the matter?"

"Ma'am, I'm trying to locate the children of Luke and Helen Purcell. I wonder . . ."

"They're my grandparents," she said at once. "Are you investigating her murder? I heard about it on television . . ."

"Yes, I am," Hawes said at once, relieved, leaning closer into the phone. "Miss Purcell, I'd like to come there to talk to you, if I may. Would there be any time this morning . . . ?"

"I'm sorry, I was just about to leave for work. Can we make it sometime tonight? I get home around five."

"Well . . . can you spare me a few minutes on the phone?"

"No, I'm sorry, I really have to go, I'm late as it is."

"Then can I come to your workplace? This is really . . ."

"No, it's a restaurant, I'm sorry. Can't you come here later today?"

"Yes, certainly," he said.

"Can you be here around five, five thirty? I should be home by then."

"Your grandparents had two children, is that right? Can you tell me . . . ?"

"I'm sorry, but I really have to go. We'll talk this evening."

"Wait!" he shouted.

"What?"

"Where are you?" he asked.

"1247 Forbes Road, Apartment 6B."

"I'll see you at five," he said.

"Five *thirty,*" she said. "I have to run. I'm sorry," she said, and hung up.

"*Damn* it!" Hawes said out loud.

Jennifer's own name was Purcell, so he figured her for either single or else divorced and using her maiden name. Either way, this meant her *father* and not her *mother* was one of the abandoned kids. He'd wanted to ask her whether the other Purcell kid was a boy or a girl. He'd wanted to ask whether she'd ever even *known* the grandmother who'd abandoned Luke and the two kids to run off with her lover. Lots of questions to ask. He couldn't wait to ask them.

He looked up at the wall clock.

Five thirty tonight seemed so very far away.

These holy, solemn, religious places gave Ollie the heebie-jeebies. Before the priest got himself killed, the last time Ollie'd been inside a church was when his sister Isabel got stranded at the altar by a no-good Jewboy grifter he'd warned her against from the very beginning, but who listens to their big brothers nowadays? He wondered, in fact, if *Patricia's* kid brother, Alonso, was warning her against Ollie himself right this very minute. As well he might be. Which was another thing that made Ollie uncomfortable about being here in Our Lady of Grace, the fact that he was actively planning, in the darkest recesses of his primeval mind, the seduction of Alonso's older sister, Patricia Gomez, a fellow police officer, no less. This coming Saturday night, no less.

All these goddamn candles.

The smell of incense.

Sunlight streaming through the stained-glass windows.

And all he could think of was taking off Patricia's panties.

Three or four religious fanatics were sitting in the pews,

praying. A guy in his fifties was polishing the big brass candlesticks behind the altar railing. Ollie walked down the center aisle like a bishop, approached the man.

"Who's in charge here?" he asked, same as he would at a crime scene.

The guy looked up, polishing rag in his right hand.

Ollie showed his detective's shield.

"Is there a head priest or something?" he asked.

The man seemed bewildered. Sparrow of a man with narrow shoulders and thin arms, blue eyes darting from the shield in Ollie's hand, to Ollie's face, and then back to the shield again. Ollie figured he wasn't playing with a full deck.

"Are you looking for Father Nealy?" the man asked.

"Sure," Ollie said. "Where do I find him?"

Father James Nealy was preparing next Sunday morning's sermon when Ollie walked into his rectory at eleven thirty that Monday morning. Ollie knew right off the man would be of no earthly help to him; he was in his early thirties, and couldn't possibly have been here at Our Lady of Grace when Father Michael was. He asked his questions, anyway.

"Did you know Father Michael personally?"

"Never met the man," Father Nealy said. "But I've heard only good things about him."

"Never heard anyone say he wished the old man was dead, right?"

Father Nealy smiled. He was wearing black trousers and a black shirt, looked like some kind of tunic. White collar.

Black, highly polished shoes. Ollie figured he had to be some kind of fag.

"No, I've never heard anyone say he wished Father Michael was dead."

"Everybody loved him, right?"

"I don't know about that. But I've heard nothing but praise from our parishioners."

"Some of them still remember him, is that it?"

"Oh yes. He was a beloved leader."

"Like I said. Everybody loved him."

"Am I detecting a mocking tone here?" Father Nealy asked. He was no longer smiling.

"No, you're detecting a detective investigating the murder of somebody everybody loved."

"I see what you mean," Father Nealy said. "Obviously, someone *didn't* love him."

"Ah yes," Ollie said. "But you wouldn't know of any friction back then when he was a priest here."

"As I said, I haven't heard of any."

"Why'd he leave here for St. Ignatius, anyway?"

"Priests are moved from one parish to another all the time," Father Nealy said. "The diocese sends us wherever we're needed to do the Lord's work."

"Of course," Ollie said, thinking, The Lord's work, what total bullshit. "Well, thanks for your time, Father," he said. "If you can think of anyone who might've had mischief on his mind, give me a call, okay? Meanwhile, may God bless you and keep you," he said, and shook hands with the priest and walked out.

He came down the long corridor that led through the

sacristy, lined with clear leaded windows streaming morning sunlight, and then back to the church proper. Inside the church, the same holy lunatics were scattered in the pews, mumbling their prayers, the same guy was behind the altar, polishing brass. He spotted Ollie the moment he came through the door into the church, almost as if he'd been waiting for him to come back.

"Detective?" he said.

Ollie turned, went to him.

"Are you investigating?" the man whispered.

Eyes wide and frightened.

"Why?" Ollie asked. "What do you know?"

"Jerry!"

A woman's voice.

Ollie turned to where a redhead going ugly gray was striding down the side aisle of the church like a witch who'd lost her broomstick.

"Leave my brother alone!" she shouted, startling the holy at prayer, and took Jerry by the hand, and dragged him away from the altar.

But this was Oliver Wendell Weeks she was dealing with here.

As brother and sister came out of the church, Ollie was right behind them.

Kling was beginning to sound to Brown like one of those tormented private eyes or rogue cops he read about in seven-dollar paperbacks that used to be dime novels that used to be penny dreadfuls. White guys mostly who went around moaning and groaning and tearing out their hair about everything but what was supposed to be their work. Their work here was supposed to be finding out who had put two bullets in Professor Christine Langston's face, plus some other faces as well.

Instead, he was telling Brown that he'd been to bed with a girl named Sadie Harris this past Friday night—another black girl, no less—whom he hadn't yet called back, but he hadn't called Sharyn again, either, and now he was asking Brown his advice on what he should do because he thought he might already be in love with this Sadie Harris, who was a librarian in Riverhead. Tell the truth, Brown didn't care whether he called Sadie *or* Sharyn, or went to bed with either or both of them, or even with Britney Spears in the window of Harrods department store in London, England. Kling's troubles with women—black women, no less—were of minor consequence to the real issue at hand, which happened to be murder. *Murders.* Plural. Five of them so far, and maybe still counting.

Of major consequence and immediate concern was Warren G. Harding High School, where a twenty-three-year-old teacher named Christine Langston had long ago given an eighteen-year-old boy a C when he'd desperately needed an A to keep him out of the Army.

What they wanted to know was the name of that boy.

But all of this was all so very long ago and very far away.

What they were talking about here was more than forty years ago. Guy would have to be in his late fifties by now. This whole damn case was buried in ancient history.

What they learned at Harding High at twelve noon that

Monday was that no one currently teaching there—*no* one—had been teaching there back then when Christine was promising A's and handing out C's instead. Nor had anyone employed in the Clerical Office today been working at the school back then.

So . . .

Either they had to admit they'd reached a dead end on the professor's murder . . .

Or else they could try some other means—God knew what—of tracking down each and every member of the graduating class back then, and all of the teachers who'd been at Harding when Christine was but a mere twenty-three, in her green and salad days, and learning how to trade grades for apparently scarce sex.

Fat Chance Department, both cops thought.

They headed back to the squadroom to discuss it with the Loot, who wasn't in such a good mood himself just then.

What goes in must come out.

What goes up must come down.

These are things you learn after years of dedicated police work.

Jerry and his sister, the graying redheaded witch, had gone into the building at 831 Barber Street at twelve-oh-seven this afternoon, and it was now twenty to one, and neither one of them had yet come out. Ollie felt certain of three things.

One: Jerry's elevator wasn't reaching the top floor; he was what the police in this city categorized as an EDP, for Emotionally Disturbed Person.

Two: Jerry believed the church was under investigation for something or other.

Three: Jerry's sister didn't want him talking to cops.

Which made talking to him seem all the more imperative.

Ollie supposed he could knock on a few doors, ask a few questions, and zero in on which apartment Jerry and his sister lived in. But then he would have to question Jerry in the presence of the harridan sister, and he would prefer not having to do that; he was still afraid of the wicked witch in *The Wizard of Oz*, and he'd seen that movie only on television. So he waited across the street from their building: What goes in must come out; what goes up must come down.

Meanwhile, all he could do was think about Patricia Gomez. Should he change their date from Saturday night to Sunday morning? Andy Parker said that a cozy little Saturday night dinner at home would set off a real Panty Block alarm. So maybe he should call her and change it to a Sunday brunch if indeed he was planning on getting in her pants, which he guessed he was, else why was he thinking such evil thoughts about the girl, and why was there a sudden erection in his own pants right this very minute?

Oh well.

It also bothered him that Andy Parker thought he was losing his essential Ollie-ness, which he certainly did not wish to do; he liked himself too much. Then again, Patricia seemed to like him a lot, too. Especially now that he'd lost ten pounds. So, when you thought about it, what would be so wrong about two consensual, nonhomosexual human beings joining together for some fine and fancy Saturday night—oops.

Here they came.

Walking out of their building together, Jerry and his sister with her graying red hair flying around her head like a halo of bats.

Alicia Hendricks's old neighborhood was beginning to feel like home to Parker and Genero. They even stopped in at Rocco's for lunch that Monday, where they had the clams Posillipo and another chat with Geoffrey Lucantonio, who was eager to tell them more about his derring-do with the then-fifteen-year-old Alicia, but they opted for other more pertinent information.

They were here in the Laurelwood section of Riverhead again, trying to track down any of Alicia's former classmates at Warren G. Harding High, which the Commish might have considered fiddling around but which nonetheless had been her last educational venue before she sailed off into the wider world of waitressing, manicuring, sales repping, and eventual dope-dealing. Geoffrey told them that not many of Harding's alumni still lived in the old hood. Although the foundation stones were still here—

Our Lady of Grace Church . . .

Roger Mercer Junior High . . .

Warren G. Harding High . . .

—the neighborhood was now predominately Spanish, and erstwhile natives of Jewish, Italian, or Irish descent had long ago fled for greener pastures. One holdout was a woman whose parents had owned a house here "when the neighborhood was still good," Geoffrey said, not recognizing he was slurring the people who currently lived here. She'd inherited the house when her parents died, and was still reluctant to give it up.

"Her name is Phoebe Jennings," he said. "Her and her husband come in here all the time. I forget what her maiden name was back then. She lives in the two-story brick behind St. Mary's."

Phoebe Jennings still bore a faint resemblance to the photo of the plain eighteen-year-old girl in Harding's yearbook. She remembered Alicia Hendricks well . . .

"Well, who could ever forget her?" she said, and rolled her eyes.

They were sitting under a striped umbrella in the backyard of the house, the yearbook open in her lap. In the near distance, the bells of St. Mary's . . .

Good title, Genero thought.

. . . chimed the hour.

It was one o'clock in the afternoon.

The way Phoebe remembers it . . .

"My maiden name was Phoebe Mears," she told the detectives. "That's the name in the yearbook there . . ."

Tapping the photo of a young girl in eyeglasses, a tentative smile on her mouth. Phoebe Jennings still wore eyeglasses, but she was not smiling as she remembered those days back in high school.

"Alicia was the most popular girl in the class," she said. "Gorgeous, drove all the boys crazy. Well, *everyone* wanted to be near her. All of us. She just radiated this . . . *glow,* you know? I realize now it was a kind of hypersexuality . . . well, we were all so young, you know, so very young."

"How well did you know her, Mrs. Jennings?" Parker asked.

"Oh, not well at *all*! I'm sorry, did I give that impression? I was hardly in the same league as Alicia and her *Chosen* Few . . . well, look at my picture. I was what kids today call a nerd. The *In* Crowd wanted nothing to do with me. This tight little circle of girls, you know, maybe five or six of them? Flocked around Alicia as if she were the queen bee. Hoping some of her *allure* would rub off on them. Well, *I* hoped so, too, I admit it. I'd have given anything to be like Alicia Hendricks. And yet . . ."

She looked at her photo in the yearbook again.

"You're here because she met with a violent death. I've been happily married for almost thirty years now. My two daughters are married, too, both of them college graduates. My husband is a decent, faithful, hardworking man, and we live a block away from the church where we worship every Sunday. So does it matter that forty years ago I was a wallflower at Our Lady of Grace's Friday night dances? Does it matter that the boys stood on line waiting for a chance to dance with Alicia or even one of her friends? Where are any of those other girls now? Are they as happy as I am?"

"Would you *know* where any of them are now, Mrs. Jennings?" Genero asked.

Holding tight to her brother's hand, the graying redhead led him up the street, Ollie a respectably invisible distance behind them. Damn if she wasn't leading him into a small coffee shop. Were the siblings about to enjoy a good lunch, which Ollie himself could use along about now? His stomach growling in agreement, he took up a watchful position across the street, and was surprised when the pair came out some ten minutes later, each carrying a brown paper bag.

He watched.

The sister kissed Jerry on the cheek. Gave him some sisterly advice, Jerry nodding. Kissed him again in farewell, and then marched off, leaving him alone on the sidewalk.

Ollie waited.

A moment later, Jerry was in motion, brown paper bag clutched tight in his right hand. Was he heading back to the apartment? If so, Ollie would follow him right upstairs this time. No sister, no problem. But instead, he walked right past his building, and kept on walking south, crossing under the elevated-train structure on Dover Plains Avenue, and then past the next street over, something called Holman Avenue, and then to the street bordering the park, and onto a footpath leading into the park itself, Ollie some fifteen feet behind him now, and rapidly closing the distance between them. The moment Jerry found a bench and sat on it, Ollie moved in. Even before Jerry could reach into the brown paper bag, Ollie was sitting beside him.

"Hello, Jerry," he said.

Jerry turned to him. Blue eyes opening wide in recognition and fear.

"I didn't do nothing," he said.

"I know you didn't," Ollie said. "What've you got there, a sandwich?"

Jerry looked puzzled for a moment. Then he realized Ollie was referring to the paper bag on his lap. "Yes," he said. "And a Coca-Cola."

"What kind of sandwich?" Ollie asked.

"Ham and cheese on a hard roll, butter and mustard," Jerry said by rote.

"Wanna share it with me?" Ollie asked. "I'll buy us a few more of them later."

"Sure," Jerry said, and grinned, and reached into the bag. He unwrapped the sandwich. The roll had already been sliced in two, which made things easy. Together, they sat on the park bench, chewing. Jerry popped the can of Coke, offered it to Ollie. Ollie took a long swallow, handed it back.

"So what is it you didn't do?" he asked.

"Nothing with the father," Jerry said, and shook his head.

"Father Nealy, you mean?"

"No. Father Michael."

Ollie nodded, bit into his half of the sandwich.

"You knew Father Michael, huh?" he asked.

"Yes. When I was small."

Forty, fifty years ago, Ollie figured. Time frame would've been right for when Father Michael was a pastor at Our Lady of Grace.

"You're investigating, right?" Jerry said.

"Investigating what, Jerry?"

"What he done to us."

"What'd he do to you, Jerry?"

"You know."

"No, I don't know. Tell me."

"To both of us."

"Uh-huh. What'd he do, Jerry? It's all right, you can tell me. He's dead now."

Jerry's blue eyes opened wide.

"He can't hurt you anymore."

"He made me and this other kid . . ."

The blue eyes welled with tears. He buried his face in his hands. Shook his head in his hands. Sobbing into his hands.

"You and another boy?"

"Not together."

"Separately?"

Jerry nodded into his hands. Mumbled *yes* into his hands.

Ollie sat still and silent for several moments.

Then he said, "What was this other boy's name?"

"Was it Carlie?" Jerry asked.

In her mid-fifties, Geraldine Davies was still an attractive woman, and the detectives could easily imagine her as one of Alicia's inner circle of friends back then in those halcyon days at Mercer Junior High and Harding High. Wearing lavender slacks and a matching cotton T-shirt, strappy low-heeled sandals, she greeted them at the door to her apartment in Majesta, offered them iced tea, and then led them out to a terrace seventeen stories above the street. There, within viewing distance of the Majesta Bridge, they sat sipping tea and enjoying the cool early afternoon breezes.

"I was always sorry I lost touch with Alicia," she told them. "She was a very important part of my life back then. Well, *all* of us. Any of us who were fortunate enough to get close to her. She was a very special person. It's a pity what happened to her. Well, getting killed the way she did, of course. But now I understand there was some sort of drug connection as well, is that right? Didn't I see on television that she was selling drugs or something, some sort of Korean connection, was it? Is that true? If so, it's a shame. She was so special."

Then why did someone want her dead? Parker wondered.

Genero said it out loud.

"Can you think of anyone back *then* who might have had reason to kill her *now*? Anyone bearing a grudge, for example?"

"Long time to be bearing a grudge," Geraldine said, and raised her eyebrows.

"Lots of nuts out there," Parker said.

"Even so."

On the bridge, even from this distance, they could hear the rumble of heavy trucks making the river crossing to Isola.

"Well, you never know, I suppose," Geraldine said, thinking.

"Yes?" Parker said.

"But there was this one boy . . ."

"Yes?"

". . . had a terrible crush on her. What was his name again?"

The detectives waited.

"I remember one night . . . at Our Lady of Grace . . . they used to have these Friday night dances at the church, they were very popular, used to draw a big crowd. This boy used to follow Alicia around like a lost puppy, panting at her heels . . . well, she was really quite beautiful, you know, I can't say I blamed him, what *was* his name?

"Anyway, this one Friday night . . . they had the dances in this huge recreation hall at the church, you know . . . well, it *seemed* huge to me, I was only thirteen. We would sit on these wooden chairs lined up against the wall, waiting for boys to ask us to dance. I have to tell you, nobody in Alicia's crowd had to wait very long. I don't want to sound conceited, but we were the most popular girls at Mercer, and later at Harding. The boys flocked around us like bees to honey. That sounds terrible, I know, but it's true.

"This one Friday night . . . this boy who everybody said had *tendencies,* you know what I mean? Like he, uh, walked *light,* you know what I mean?"

She was suddenly a teenager again.

And not a very nice one, they realized.

Smiling now, remembering, she told of how this boy with *tendencies* came walking across the entire long length of this *huge* recreation hall, and stopped in front of where Alicia and she were laughing at something one of them had just said . . .

"She was wearing a yellow dress, I remember, ruffled, short to show off her legs, she had terrific legs, well, listen, she was just a terrific girl . . .

". . . and he asked her to dance . . . *what* was his name, I can't *imagine* what's wrong with my memory these days! Held out his hand to her. 'Would you care to dance?' he said, such a wuss. Alicia looked up at him. Ray Charles was on the record player, I remember now. Looked him dead in the eye. Said, 'Get lost, faggot.' Which he deserved. I mean, everybody *said* he was.

"He just turned and walked away. But you should have seen the look on his face. If looks could kill . . ."

Geraldine shook her head.

"Walked that whole long distance back across the rec hall again, went out the door, and out of the church for all I know. Never followed Alicia around again, you can bet on that. Never. I wonder whatever happened to him. Such a wuss. I can't even remember his name."

"Mrs. Jennings," Parker said, "*try* to remember his name."

"Chuck something?" she said.

9.

The Department of Veterans Affairs provided a list of local Vietnam vets who'd served in either D Company (or perhaps B Company, depending on which relative you believed) of the 2nd Brigade of the 25th Infantry Division during Operation Ala Moana. But getting a straight story from any of them wasn't as easy as Meyer and Carella had hoped.

Some were reluctant to talk about the worst experience they'd ever had in their lives. All of them were remembering events that had taken place close to forty years ago. Obscured by the fog of war, separate encounters took on almost surreal significance . . .

". . . the jungles in Nau Nghia Province are thick and dense, you never know who's behind what tree, you can't tell which trail Charlie has already booby-trapped . . ."

". . . Max Sobolov, yeah, he was our sergeant. And it was D Company, D for Dog, not B, you got that wrong . . ."

"This was only thirty miles northwest of Saigon, but you'd think you were in the heart of Africa someplace . . ."

". . . something to do with a Vietnamese woman, Sobolov and this kid in his squad. They were taking her back for questioning . . ."

". . . the stuff was stashed in this village, these huts they had, you know? Buried in these huts. AT mines, and rice, and sugar, and pickled fish, all there for Charlie to use whenever he dropped in . . ."

Mark was in his room watching television when Teddy walked in on him at four o'clock that Monday afternoon. April was at a sleepover; Teddy felt perfectly safe talking to her son. She went immediately to the television set, turned it off, stood in front of the screen facing him, and began signing at once, as if she'd been preparing for this a long while, the words tumbling from her hands in a rush.

Your father and I have been talking, she signed. *You have to tell us what's going on.*

"Nothing, Mom."

Then why'd you burst into tears on the way home from practice yesterday?

"It's just that April and I aren't as close anymore," he said, "that's all. Mom, really, it's nothing."

Then why couldn't you just tell that to Dad?

"April and I need to work it out for ourselves," Mark said, and shrugged. "Kids, you know?" he said, and tried a lame smile.

Teddy looked him dead in the eye.

There's something you're not telling us, she signed. *What is it, Mark?*

"Nothing."

Has her friend stolen something else?

"No. I don't know. April hasn't said anything about . . ."

Because if that girl is a thief . . .

"It isn't that, Mom."

Then what the hell is it, Mark! Teddy signed, her eyes blazing, her fingers flying. *Tell me right this minute!*

Mark hesitated.

M-a-a-rk, she signed, her hands stretching the simple word into a warning.

"They were doing pot," he said.

Who?

Eyes and fingers snapping.

"Lorraine and the older boys."

Where?

"At the party last Tuesday. Some of the other girls, too."

April? Teddy asked at once.

"I don't know. They were all in Lorraine's bedroom. The door was locked."

Was April in there with them?

Again, he hesitated.

Was she?

"Yes, Mom."

Are you sure about this, Mark?

"I know what it smells like, Mom."

Teddy nodded.

Thanks, son, she signed.

"Did I just get her in trouble again?" Mark asked.

No, you just got her out *of it,* Teddy signed, and hugged her son close, and kissed the top of his head.

Then she went directly into her own bedroom, and opened her laptop there, and immediately e-mailed her husband at work.

"Patricia?"

"Hey, hi, Oll!"

"How you doing?"

"Great. I just got home a few minutes ago. Whussup?"

"I've been doing some thinking. You know, it's been frantic here, these Glock murders . . ."

"Oh, I'll bet."

"So I thought . . . let me try this on you . . . I may not have the time to go shopping for the kind of dinner I'd like to make for you this Saturday . . ."

"Oh sure, Oll. You want to make it some other night?"

"Well, not exactly. I thought if you could come over here

for brunch Sunday *morning*... instead of dinner the night *before*... it would be a lot simpler. I could make pancakes for us..."

"Yummy, I love pancakes. But that's the Fourth, isn't it? Sunday?"

"Yes," he said, suddenly thinking he was making a wrong move here. "Yes, it is. Will that be a problem?"

"No, no. In fact, we could hang out together all day, and then go see the fireworks at night."

"That's just what I thought. We'd make it real casual, you know. Blue jeans. Like that."

"Sounds good to me," Patricia said. "Just a nice, easy, relaxed Sunday."

"And fireworks later," Ollie reminded her.

"Lo-fat pancakes, though, right?"

"Right, lo-fat."

"Terrific. Good idea, Oll. What time did you have in mind?"

"Eleven o'clock all right?"

"Perfect. I'll see you then."

"Good," he said. "Good, Patricia. Casual, right? Blue jeans."

"Blue jeans, got it. See you then."

"See you, Patricia," he said, and hung up.

His heart was pounding.

He felt as if he'd just planned a candy store holdup.

On and on the veterans' stories went...

"*... this wasn't my squad, it was another squad in D Company. You know how this works? Or do you? There's your* *company, has two to four platoons in it, and then there's your platoon, has two to four squads. There are only nine, ten soldiers in a squad, you get it? This kid who shot the woman was in another squad . . ."*

". . . we flushed out seven bunkers and two tunnels in the area just to the rear of us. Captured twelve 81-millimeter rounds and 11,200 small-arms rounds, more than a ton of rice, and a Russian-made radio . . ."

". . . an encircling maneuver, like in a vil sweep, we done them all the time. Attack at first light, catch Charlie by surprise. But they knew we were coming, they'd lined the trail with rifles and machine guns, and we walked right into it . . ."

". . . Sobolov took a mortar explosion should've killed him. Instead, it only blinded him."

It wasn't until that Monday afternoon, at a little past five o'clock, that Meyer and Carella located the lieutenant who'd been in command of the almost two hundred men in D Company during the Ala Moana offensive in December of 1966, almost thirty-nine years ago. His name was Danny Freund. Now sixty-one, with graying hair and a noticeable limp . . .

"My war souvenir," he told them.

. . . he was enjoying a day away from his law office, supervising his two grandchildren in the park. On nearby swings, the kids reached for the sky while Freund recalled a time he'd much rather have forgotten.

"I don't know what you've learned about Sobolov," he said, "but there aren't many of us lamenting his murder, I can tell you that. He was your stereotypical top sergeant, believe me. A complete son of a bitch."

"Some of the men in your company mentioned an incident with a Vietnamese woman," Meyer said. "What was that all about?"

"It was all about a court martial that never happened. Max brought this kid up on . . ."

"What kid?"

"Twenty-year-old kid in his squad. Blew a Vietnamese woman away. Sobolov brought charges on an Article 32. That's the equivalent of a civilian grand jury. Convened to determine if a crime was committed and if it's reasonable to assume the person charged committed the crime. The kid claimed he'd been ordered to shoot the woman. Claimed Sobolov had ordered him to do it. The judges refused to take the matter to the next step. Instead, they . . ."

"The next step?"

"They refused to recommend a court martial."

"So they ruled in favor of the kid, right?" Carella said.

"Well, that depends on how you look at it, I guess. Conviction in a court martial would have meant a punitive discharge. Either a DD or a BCD. Instead, the judges ruled . . ."

He saw the puzzled looks on their faces.

"Dishonorable Discharge," he explained. "Bad Conduct Discharge. Either one would have meant a serious loss of benefits. Instead, the kid got what's called an OTH—an Other Than Honorable discharge. The OTH entailed a loss of benefits, too. Most significantly the GI Bill—which would have paid for his college education."

Freund shook his head, cast an eye on his soaring grandchildren, yelled, "Boys! Time to go!" and rose from the bench. "Sobolov got off scot-free," he said. "Well, maybe not. He came out of the war blind. But if, in fact, he gave the order that took that young woman's life, he deserved whatever he got. Even before Ala Moana, he was smoking pot day and night. Couldn't function without his daily toke. A bully, a prick, and a hophead, that's what Sergeant Max Sobolov was. When that mortar shell took his eyes, everyone in the platoon cheered. We'd have cheered louder if it had killed him."

"This soldier he brought up on charges," Meyer said. "Would you remember his name?"

"Charlie Something. Like the enemy."

"Charlie what?"

"Let me think a minute," Freund said, and started walking toward the swings, the detectives beside him. "Oh, sure," he said, "it was . . ."

Jennifer Purcell lived in a low-rise apartment building in what used to be an Italian neighborhood in Riverhead. Now largely Puerto Rican, the area was enjoying a sort of vogue among younger people because of its proximity to the city proper: Forbes Avenue was a scant twenty minutes by subway to the heart of downtown Isola.

At five thirty that Monday, Jennifer admitted Hawes to her apartment and immediately apologized for its messy appearance. "I work the day shift on Mondays," she said, "we get a big lunch crowd. I haven't had a chance to tidy up yet." She further explained that she was a waitress at a restaurant called Paulie's downtown, and apologized again for not being able to talk to him this morning, but she was truly on her way out when he called.

She was, as Hawes had surmised from her telephone voice, a woman in her late twenties. Wearing jeans and a cotton sweater, her brown hair pulled back into a ponytail, no makeup, not even lipstick. Plain. A trifle overweight. They sat at her kitchen table, drinking coffee.

"Do you think you'll find who killed her?" she asked.

"We're working on it," Hawes said.

"The newspapers are saying it was a serial killer. That she was just another random victim."

"Well, the newspapers," he said.

"I've been following the case. Not because she's my grandmother. In fact, I never met the woman. She just up and left, you know. Never even tried to contact her own children again. That's odd, don't you think? A woman leaving her own children that way? Ten and eight years old? Never trying to reach them again? Talk to them even? I think that's very odd. My father despised her."

"Was he the oldest? Or the youngest?"

"The oldest. He was ten when she left."

"Is he still alive?"

"No, he died of cancer twelve years ago, when he was forty-eight. That's very young. It runs in the family, you know. My grandfather died of cancer, too. Luke. He was much older, though, this was only seven years ago. He was seventy-six years old. I blame it all on her."

"On . . . ?"

"My grandmother. Helen. Leaving them the way she did. Cancer is directly traceable to stress, you know. My grandfather was a young man when she left the family, thirty-three, that's very young. The boys were only ten and eight. He raised them alone, a single father, never remarried. The boys were very close when they were young . . . well, you can imagine, no mother. Then . . . well . . . my father died so young, you know. I didn't see much of my uncle after that. He just sort of . . . drifted away."

"Is your mother still alive?"

"Oh yes. Remarried, in fact. Living in Florida. A Jewish man." She hesitated a moment, looked down at her hands folded in her lap now. "There's not much of a family anymore, I suppose. I'm an only child, you know. The last time I saw my uncle was when he came to my grandfather's funeral seven years ago. He seemed so . . . I don't know . . . distant. He never married, bought himself a little house out on Sands Spit. He was working in a shoe store then, selling shoes. He was always a salesman, ever since he got out of the Army. He was in Vietnam, you know. He used to sell records after the war. In a music store, you know. He used to bring me records all the time. I liked him a lot. I think she did everyone great harm back then. I don't think any of them ever recovered from it. Well, cancer killed two of them.

That's stress, you know. Cancer. Helen Reilly. I didn't even know her name until I read about her murder in the paper. I mean, I didn't know this was my own *grandmother* until I read she was the former Helen Purcell. Then it clicked. And . . . I have to tell you . . . I was glad. I was glad someone killed her."

The small kitchen went silent.

"I know that's a terrible thing to say, may God forgive me. But it's what I felt."

"Have you talked to your uncle about it?"

"About . . . ?"

"His mother's death. Helen Reilly's death."

"No. I told you, the last time I saw him . . ."

"Yes, but I thought you might have spoken afterward. When you heard about the murder . . ."

"No."

"Would you know where I can reach him?"

"No. I'm sorry. I think he still lives out on the Spit, but I don't have the address, I'm sorry."

"Can you tell me his name?" Hawes said.

"My uncle's name? Well, of *course* I . . ."

"I know it's Purcell," Hawes said. "But what's his first name?"

"Charles," she said. "Uncle Charles."

Carella had just finished reading Teddy's e-mail when the phone on his desk rang. He sat stunned and shocked for a moment, staring at his computer screen, before reaching for the receiver.

"Eighty-seventh Squad," he said. "Carella."

"Steve?"

Faint accent.

"Who's this, please?" he said.

"Il tuo patrigno," the voice said. "Your stepfather. Luigi."

"Is something wrong?" Carella said at once.

"*Qualcosa non va*? No, what could be wrong? Am I calling at a bad time? What time is it there?"

"Almost six," Carella said.

"It's almost midnight here," Luigi said. "Your mother's already asleep."

Carella waited. *Was* something wrong? Why this call from Milan? Where it was almost midnight.

"Is she okay?" he asked. "Mom."

"Yes, fine. She met me for lunch in town today, and then she went shopping. She came home exhausted. We had a late dinner and she went straight to bed." He hesitated. "I thought I'd call to see *come va,* how everything it goes there. I'm not bothering you, am I?"

"No, no. Bothering me? No. Shopping for what?"

"Things we still need for the apartment. Not furniture, I *manufacture* furniture, we have furniture up to our eyeballs, is how you say it? But towels, sheets, pots and pans, all that. We bought this new apartment, you know . . ."

We, Carella noticed. *We* bought this new apartment. Not *I* bought it. He considered this a good sign. A partnership. Like his own with Teddy.

". . . on the Via Ariosto, near the park. Eight rooms, plenty for when you and the children come to visit, eh? Also, this weekend, we'll be driving to Como to look at a rental for the summer—if it's not already too late to get one. The lake is about an hour from here, I'll be able to go there for weekends and for the entire month of August, when I take my holiday from the office. Which would be a good time for you to visit with the children, no? It will be big enough for all of us, I'll make sure, something nice on the lake, eh? How *are* the children, Steve?"

Carella hesitated.

"Fine," he said at last. "Well, they're teenagers now, you know. Their birthday was a week ago."

"Did you get what Luisa and I sent? Mama and I?"

"No, not yet."

"*Madonna, ma com'è possibile?* We sent their gifts by courier! I will have my secretary check. Not there yet? *Ma che idioti!*"

"I'll call when they arrive, don't worry," Carella said.

There was a short silence on the line.

"What did you mean, I know about teenagers?" Luigi asked. "Is something the matter?"

"Well, you know."

"Tell me."

The identical words Carella used when interrogating a perp. Tell me.

"Well, you have children, you know."

"I have children with teenagers of their *own*!" Luigi said. "What's the matter, Steve?"

And then, just the way a perp will often take a deep breath before blurting that he'd killed his wife and their pet canary with a hatchet, Carella took a deep breath and said, "April's smoking marijuana."

"Oh, *madonna!*" Luigi said. "When did this happen?"

"I just found out this minute. Did you ever have such trouble? When your kids were small?"

He still thought of April as "small." Lipstick. High heels. Small. But thirteen. And smoking marijuana.

"Yes. Well, not dope, no, although there is plenty of that here, too," Luigi said. "But yes, when Annamaria was fourteen, she started running with a bad crowd, is that how you say it? *Un brutto giro?*"

"A bad crowd, yes."

"Alcohol, wild parties, everything. Fourteen years old! My baby!"

"Yes," Carella said. "That's just it, Luigi."

"You must talk to April at once. You must let her know this will not be tolerated in our family."

"Is that what you did?"

"The very moment I learned what was happening. We would not let her out of the house for a month. Not until she got herself loose of these bad people. I told her I would call the police! But you *are* a police, no, Steve? Tell her. This will not be tolerated! Our family will not be shamed this way! Luisa would die! Shall I tell her? Do you want me to tell her, Steve? *Figliolo,* may I tell Mama?"

Figliolo, Carella thought. Son, he thought. May I tell Mama?

"Not yet, Luigi, please," he said. "Let me call you after we've talked to April. Be better that way."

"*Si, meglio così.* I will wait for your call. Give my love to Teddy. Let me know what happens. Please."

"I promise."

"Allora, ci sentiamo presto," Luigi said, and hung up.

"Thanks . . ." Carella started, but the line had already gone dead and there was only a dial tone.

He'd almost said, Thanks, Pop.

Well, next time, he thought.

He tried the words silently.

Thanks, Pop.

Then, aloud into the dead phone, he said, "Thanks, Pop," and then, louder, "Thanks, Papa," and replaced the phone gently on its receiver.

When the limo didn't show up by six fifteen, Charles Purcell went back into the lobby and asked the concierge to dial the car company's number for him. The dispatcher he spoke to told him that the car had got caught in heavy traffic near the Calm's Point Bridge . . .

"Well, where is he now?" he asked.

"Just coming off the Drive, sir."

Charles looked at his watch.

"Then cancel it," he said. "I'll take a taxi."

"I'm sorry, sir, we . . ."

"That's all right, another time," he said, and hung up. He went directly out of the hotel to the curb, where he asked the doorman to hail a cab for him. Once seated inside, he gave the driver Reggie's address on North Hastings and told him there'd be a twenty-dollar tip for him if he got there before six thirty. He looked at his watch again. The driver pulled away from the curb in a screech of rubber.

Charles had made the dinner reservation for six thirty, but

now he figured they'd be fifteen or so minutes late, that damn limo company. Well, still time enough, maybe, the way the cabbie was weaving his way in and out of traffic. Amazing what the promise of a little money could do. He was rather getting used to this lifestyle. Pity it wouldn't last forever, but then again, nothing ever did.

She was waiting on the steps outside her building when the taxi pulled up. Charles asked the driver to keep the meter running, and then he got out of the car and was walking toward her, a grin on his face, when all at once everything seemed to happen in a rush. In that single instant, he was transported back to Nam, the way in Nam things suddenly erupted everywhere around you, and you didn't realize at first that this was really happening to you, that this attack was directed at you.

The man who seemed to materialize out of nowhere was perhaps six feet tall, with wide shoulders and a massive chest, a six-hundred-pound gorilla wearing jeans and a black T-shirt, black running shoes, striding toward where Reggie was standing on the front steps of her building, turned away from him, looking at Charles as he approached from the opposite direction, a smile forming on her mouth when she recognized him and started down the steps. Just then the man in the black T-shirt seized her right wrist, and yanked her full off the steps and onto the sidewalk. As Charles watched in shocked disbelief, the man smacked her across the face, so hard that she would have fallen over backward had he not been holding tight to her wrist.

"Lost your way?" he asked sweetly, and smacked her again.

"*You!*" Charles yelled, pointing his finger at him. In the

next instant, he was running toward the man, who was now dragging Reggie behind him on the sidewalk. She was wearing a shiny silver dress, cut high on the thigh, high-heeled, silver-toned, patent-leather slippers. She dug in her heels, resisting, but the man had her tight by the wrist, and when she tried to pull away, he smacked her again, and then again. By this time, Charles was on him.

"Oh?" the man said, and shook Charles off like a dog shedding water. Charles rushed him again. The man hit him full in the face, hard. His nose began spurting blood. "You son of a bitch!" Reggie yelled, and yanked off one of the silver-toned slippers and swung the heel at his head. The man brushed the blow aside. He was bringing back his arm to hit Reggie again, when suddenly he saw the gun in Charles's hand.

"Hey now," he cautioned, but Charles was already firing.

Reggie screamed.

Charles kept firing until the gun was empty.

The taxi roared away from the curb.

"Oh Jesus," Reggie whispered.

Charles grabbed her hand.

Together, they ran off into the night.

The brilliant fiddlers of the Eighty-seventh Squad were burning the midnight oil. More accurately, it was now 12:02 A.M. on Tuesday morning, the twenty-ninth of June, and they were burning with the need to tell each other how clever they'd been in coming up with a name for the guy they suspected had drilled five victims with the same nine-millimeter Glock. Yes, they had all, each and separately, come up with a name, ta-ra! Or *variations* on a name, actually, but certainly one and the same name; whether it was Carlie, Chuck, or Charlie, the given name was undoubtedly Charles, and the surname most definitely was Purcell.

But more than that—and Hawes took credit for this one, because it was Jennifer Purcell who'd told him her uncle Charles might still be living out on Sands Spit—they found a telephone listing for a Charles Purcell in a little town called Oatesville, not an hour outside the city in Russell County. Their law enforcement directory gave them a listing for the Sheriff's Department in Russell County. Hawes made the call, speaking to a deputy sheriff named Lyall Farr, and requesting a 410 Graham Lane drive-by, with a P&D on Charles Purcell, murder suspect. Farr said they'd do the courtesy pick-up, but delivery to the city was out of the question as Russell was extremely shorthanded at the moment. Hawes settled for a Pick-Up and Hold. Twenty minutes later, Farr called back to say the house was dark and locked, so what now? Hawes told him to break in, there was a murder suspect living there. Farr told Hawes there was no way Russell would break in without a No-Knock warrant. Besides, the next-door neighbor had seen Purcell leaving with a suitcase at the beginning of the month, said he planned to spend some time in the city.

"House has been empty since then," Farr told him.

"In the city *where*?" Hawes asked.

"I don't follow."

"Spending some time *where* in the city?"

"Didn't say. Looks to me like you're a day late and a dollar short."

Or so it seemed until the phone call came at 12:47 A.M., from a Detective David Bannerman of the Eighty-sixth Squad, not two miles away from the old Eight-Seven.

Bannerman told them that at first it had looked like a Domestic Dispute. Lady taking the air on the front steps of her building, husband or boyfriend walks up to her, starts yelling at her, slapping her around. Family quarrel, pure and simple, something for routine handling by the blues on patrol.

Then all at once it turned into something else. Guy getting out of a taxi pulls a gun, goes after the goon doing the slapping, empties the gun into him. Seventeen slugs, leaves the goon looking like Swiss cheese on the sidewalk. So now this is beginning to have all the earmarks of a *gangland* slaying, right? You empty a gun into somebody? You want to make sure he's dead, right? Also, the goon turns out to have a record goes back to when he's still a juve, this has to be gang shit, correct?

"We got a description of the shooter from one of the witnesses," Bannerman said. "He was about six feet tall, slender, wearing a dark blue suit and a tie. He was bald. Entirely bald. No sideburns, nothing. Witness said he looked very white. Pale. Almost Oriental. Or ascetic, was her exact word. Pale and ascetic. Like a holy man. The Dalai Lama? She referred to the Dalai Lama, you know what he looks like? Neither do I. But like that. A holy man."

"Some holy man," Carella said.

He was wondering why Bannerman was giving him this long song and dance.

"So we figured some wiseguy went after this Benjamin Bugliosi—is the vic's name—and did him in good. But that was before Ballistics called ten minutes ago . . ."

Uh-oh, Carella thought.

". . . and told us the gun used to dust Bugliosi was the same Model 17 used in the five homicides you guys are already investigating. So FMU prevails, pal, and you now got yourselves *six* vics—which rhymes when you come to think of it. Mazel tov."

"Thanks," Carella said.

The clock on the squadroom wall now read 1:27 A.M.

As revealed on the computer, Benjamin "The Bug" Bugliosi's B-sheet listed his first offense as a simple assault when he was sixteen. Kindly, understanding judge, suspended sentence. His most recent brush with the law—his twelfth, by the way—was six years ago, another assault this time, aggravated this time. Seems he'd been working as a bouncer for a private "club" called Sophisticates, a thinly disguised whore house cum escort service, when a drunk and obstreperous client tried to insert the muzzle of a pistol into the vagina of one of the club's virginal maidens. Bugliosi threw the man down the stairs and then repeatedly banged his head against the foyer wall before heaving him out onto the sidewalk and kicking his head to a bloody pulp. In the rain, no less. Tsk-tsk. No wonder he'd subsequently served time at Castleview Prison upstate.

The record further revealed that he'd been paroled last November, was apparently gainfully employed again, and was dutifully reporting for each of his scheduled parole-office visits. The parole office was closed at this hour, and would not open again till nine in the morning. The FBI profile on serial killers maintained that the murders only grew more vicious as time went by . . .

(Seventeen slugs this time around.)

If Purcell was indeed a serial killer . . .

(There were now six vics.)

"Let's see if Bugliosi went back to work for Sophisticates," Carella said.

It had been a long while since either Carella or Meyer had been inside a whore house at two thirty in the morning. Sophisticates occupied the entire four-story building on a quiet midtown side street. It had begun raining lightly by the time the detectives announced themselves over a wall-speaker set in the doorjamb downstairs, giving everybody upstairs an opportunity to pull up his pants or put on her panties; they weren't here looking for a vice bust. Indeed, everything appeared decorous and in fact almost homey when after a ten-minute wait they were allowed into the lobby and then upstairs to the waiting room, where black, white, Latina, and Asian ladies lounged about in negligees and lacy lingerie, but where nary a soul could be seen copulating or doing any other such dirty thing.

One of the girls was truly beautiful. Tall blonde girl in her mid-twenties, they guessed, wearing a black silk robe open over risky tap pants and skimpy bra, beamed them a big welcoming smile when they came in, even though she had to know they were cops. Carella wondered what the hell she was doing in a whore house—not that you'd guess this was one, with its smoky mirrored walls, and its tufted velveteen banquettes. Looked more like a lounge in a hotel lobby. In fact, the only male in evidence was a big black dude who introduced himself as Roger, and said he was the night manager here at Sophisticates, would the gentlemen care for a cup of coffee?

"Benjamin Bugliosi," Meyer said.

"Benny the Bug," Carella said.

Roger looked blank.

"Does he work here?"

"Not on my watch."

"Whose then?"

"Don't believe I know the man," Roger said.

"Would you know where he might have been last night around six thirty?"

"I come on at midnight," Roger said.

"We're looking for whoever might've killed him at that time."

"Oh dear," Roger said.

"Tall white guy, bald as I am," Meyer said.

"Wouldn't know him, either," Roger said.

"I know them both," the good-looking blonde said.

"Shut up, cunt," Roger told her.

"They sent him . . ."

"I *said* shut up," Roger said, and moved on her.

"Hold it," Meyer said, and slammed the flat of his hand against Roger's chest. Roger bunched his fists, and his eyes glared, but he stopped dead in his tracks.

"What's your name, miss?" Carella said.

"Trish," she said.

She told them that two weeks ago, it must've been . . .

"You lose track of time up here. Was it two weeks ago? Around then, anyway. Me and this other girl who works here, Regina—that's her real name—went on an all-night out-call to this bald guy you were telling Roger about, looked like a monk or something, no hair at all, no eyebrows, no eyelashes, nothing. Hung like a stallion, but no hair, strange. We were there with him all night, this was a Thursday night, the nineteenth, was it? Is that two weeks ago? What's today, anyway?"

"It's the twenty-ninth," Carella said.

"Already?"

"All day," he said.

They were sitting in Roger's office, the door closed. She kept glancing over her shoulder at the closed door, afraid it would open and Roger would be standing there, telling her to shut up, cunt.

"So it was less than two weeks," Trish said, and shrugged. The silk robe fell free of her shoulder. Idly, she moved it back into place. "Anyway, Regina doesn't show up for work here after that night. Called in to say she just got the Curse, but then nothing after that, silence. Sophisticates don't go for freelancing, you know what I mean? So I heard them telling the Bug to go find her, teach her a lesson. I tried to call her, warn her, but she wasn't answering the phone, and her machine wasn't on, either, which is strange for a hooker. A telephone is a hooker's lifeline, you know what I mean? So I figured she'd made some kind of private arrangement with Baldy, he was throwin money around like it was goin out of style. Did he hurt her bad, the Bug?"

"We don't know," Meyer said.

"I hope not," she said, and shrugged again. The robe fell free again. This time, she did not bother to adjust it. "I better not come back here no more, huh?" she said, and looked over her shoulder at the closed door.

"This out-call on the nineteenth, you said it was," Carella said.

"Around then, yeah."

"What was the man's name, would you remember?"

"Charles," she said.

"Charles what?"

"Didn't say. They never do."

"Where was it?"

"The Albemarle Hotel. Downtown on Holman."

She glanced at the closed door again. Sitting with her robe open, her breasts exposed in their skimpy black bra, her hands folded in her lap, she suddenly looked as forlorn as a six-year-old whose lollipop had fallen into the sandbox.

"Can I walk down with you guys when you leave?" she asked.

"Nobody ever did anything like that for me in my entire life," Reggie said.

She was cuddled in his arms in the big king-sized bed in the master bedroom of the executive suite on the fourteenth floor of the Albemarle Hotel, the same big bed they'd been sleeping in together for the past it seemed forever now. They were both naked. It was almost three in the morning; they'd made love the moment they got back here to the hotel, and they'd been talking since.

"My hero," she said.

"Some hero," he said. But he was pleased.

"He could've killed me."

"I thought he was going to."

"Dead-Eye Dick here," she said, and grinned. "I love you so much, Chaz."

"I love you, too, Reg."

"You *killed* a man for me!" she said.

"Not so loud," he warned playfully.

"Did you ever kill anyone before? I know you were in Vietnam . . ."

"I killed five other people since the sixteenth of June," he said.

"Get out!"

"The Glock Murders? You read about them? That's me."

"You'll give me a heart attack!"

"No, no, please . . ."

"Are you serious?"

"Cross my heart."

"Get out," she said again.

"I mean it," he said. "Counting that man last night, I've already killed six people in this city."

"And here I thought I was special," she said, and kissed him teasingly on the mouth. "Why'd you kill all these people, Chaz?"

"I killed the man last night because he was hurting you," he said.

"Maybe I *am* special," she said, and kissed him again, more seriously this time. "And the others?"

"Because they hurt me."

"I better never hurt you," she said.

"I know you never would."

"Never," she said, and looked into his face, his eyes, studied his mouth, touched his cheek. "So now we better get out of here, right? Cause you're a wanted desperado here, right?"

"There isn't much time," he said.

"Come on, there's *plenty* of time! Would you like to go to Mexico?"

"Mexico would be nice," he said.

She nodded into his shoulder. She was silent for a while. He held her close.

"So maybe we could go to Mexico," she said.

"Wherever you like."

"Does it bother you I'm a hooker?"

"You're not a hooker, Reg."

She nodded again.

"Maybe I'm not," she said.

There was some sort of commotion in the main room outside. They both sat up in bed just as six detectives in Kevlar vests burst into the bedroom, guns drawn. Some guy in tails and striped trousers stood behind them, a passkey in his hand, looking very frightened. Charles reached at once for the Glock on the bedside table.

"Don't touch it, Baldy!" Meyer yelled.

Talk about the pot calling the kettle.

10.

Seemed like old times.

The good old days, y'know?

Back when strangers were killing strangers for no reason at all.

In recent years, the murder rate in this city had dropped to less than two a day. That was progress. Last year by this time, 307 people had been killed; since January of this year, the total was only 273. But that didn't count the eleven people—including Benjamin Bugliosi—who'd been killed last night in what the early editions of the tabloids were already calling MONDAY, BLOODY MONDAY!

Since six thirty last night, when Bugliosi was shot and killed outside 753 North Hastings, there had been six killings in Calm's Point, one in Majesta, and three in the Laurelwood section of Riverhead. One of the Riverhead victims had been stabbed in the chest while struggling to prevent the theft of a white-gold chain and cross he wore around his neck. The victim in Majesta had been shot in the stomach. His seventeen-year-old assailant had fled into a subway station, and, when pursued from there by police, had run into an alley off Dunready Street, where he'd shot himself in the head.

Except for the arrest in the Bugliosi case, there'd been no others. But the DA's Office was on high alert, and any one of half a dozen assistant DAs could have answered the Q&A call from the Eight-Seven. It was sheer luck of the draw that caused Nellie Brand to trot all the way uptown at four A.M. that Tuesday morning.

"Thing is," Carella was telling her, "he doesn't seem to give a damn. That we caught him."

"Has he admitted killing all six of them?" Nellie asked.

She'd been on rotation since midnight, but she looked fresh and alert in a beige linen suit and lime-colored blouse. Blonde hair trimmed close. Lipstick, no other makeup.

"All six," Carella said. "But he says the last one was self-defense. Says he was defending his fiancée."

"His fiancée, huh? What about her?" Nellie said.

"We're not looking for a 230 bust," Carella said. "We're letting her go."

"So when do we talk to him?"

"Soon as the video guy gets here."

It was now ten minutes past four.

The Q&A started at 4:32 A.M.

By that time, the technician had set up his video equipment and was ready to tape the proceedings. The technician had taped hundreds of these Q&As before, and was frankly bored to tears by most of them. Every now and then you got something juicy like a guy drooling to tell you how he'd enjoyed stabbing a woman fifteen times in her left breast and then drinking blood from her nipple afterward, which to tell the truth the video guy had found sort of exciting, too. But most of the time, you got mundane motives for murder, which was alliterative but not too terribly thrilling. The video guy could barely stifle a yawn as Charles Purcell was sworn in, was read his rights yet another time, and was then asked for the record to tell his name and current address, which he gave as 410 Graham Lane in Oatesville. Nellie stepped in.

Q: Mr. Purcell, as I understand this, you have refused counsel, is that correct?

A: I don't need a lawyer.

Q: You realize, do you not . . . ?

A: I don't need a lawyer.

Q: Will you please confirm for the record that you have been advised of your rights to counsel, and have refused it, and are now willing to answer my questions *without* presence of counsel?

A: Yes. All of that. Let's get on with it.

Q: Mr. Purcell, where were you last night at about six thirty P.M.?
A: I was picking up my fiancée. We were . . .
Q: By your fiancée . . .
A: Regina Marshall. She lives at 753 North Hastings. We were supposed to go to dinner together. She had gone home to change her clothes. She was waiting downstairs for me when she was attacked by the man I shot in self-defense.
Q: Benjamin Bugliosi?
A: I was later told his name, yes. I had no idea who he was when I shot him. All I knew was that he was hurting Reggie.
Q: Does the name Michael Hopwell mean anything to you?
A: Yes, he's the priest I killed.
Q: Christine Langston?
A: Yes, I killed her, too.
Q: Alicia Hendricks?
A: Yes.
Q: Max Sobolov?
A: Yes, I killed him.
Q: Helen Reilly? Did you kill her as well?
A: I killed them all.
Q: Why did you kill these people?
A: They fiddled with my life.
Q: I'm sorry, they . . . ?
A: They fucked up my life.

It was 4:39 A.M. when he started telling them. The sun was just coming up. A golden light splashed through the barred squadroom windows, but it did not reach the windowless interrogation room where Charles Purcell was telling them why he'd killed the five people he felt had ruined his life. His recitation did not end until 5:32 A.M., when he finished telling them he'd killed Max Sobolov because his wartime sergeant had been responsible for his OTH discharge from the army.

"I couldn't go to college because of him," he said.

The room went still except for the almost soundless whir of the camera.

Nellie looked around the room at the gathered detectives.

"Anyone?" she said. "Anything?"

"Can you go over them one more time?" Ollie said. "In order this time?"

He went through each and every murder yet another time, chronologically in present time, and then chronologically in past time as well. He was eight and called Carlie when his mother abandoned the family . . .

I had my own key, I let myself into the apartment. My father was at work, my brother had basketball practice after school, but my mother should have been home. The house was so still. Sunlight coming through the windows. The clock ticking.

I went to the fridge to get myself a glass of milk and some cookies. My mother always had a snack prepared for us when we got home from school.

There was a note on the refrigerator door.

Hand lettered.

Dear Andrew and Carlie . . .

I couldn't pronounce "Charlie" back then, I was only eight.

Dear Andrew and Carlie . . .

Forgive me for this, but I must leave without you. He does not want your father's children.

One day you will understand.

Mom

I thought, Who *does not want my father's children?*

Who *does not want Andy and me?*

I thought, Understand what?

There wasn't any milk or cookies in the fridge.

"You killed your own fucking mother," Parker said.

"She stopped being my mother when I was eight."

He was ten and still called Carlie when the priest molested him . . .

It wasn't like behind closed doors or anything, no covert nook in some secret cloister, no dark corner with vaulting arches and windows streaming fractured light, no solemn silent afternoon seduction.

This was in broad daylight.

On the front seat of a Chrysler convertible.

The top down.

Sunshine everywhere.

Insects buzzing in the road in the fields on either side of the little dirt road.

I was ten years old.

"Now, isn't this nice, Carlie? A ride in the country? Isn't this lovely?"

"Look, Carlie."

"No, here, Carlie."

"Look at my lap."

"Do you see, Carlie?"

"No, don't be afraid."

"Touch it, Carlie."

The insects buzzing.

"Yes, Carlie. That's a good boy, Carlie."

His hand on my head.

Guiding me.

Leading me.

"It wouldn't have happened if I still had a mother," he told them.

He was fourteen-year-old Chuck when a thirteen-year-old beauty refused to dance with him . . .

The church was this big yellow stucco building on the corner of Laurelwood and I forget which cross street. Dominated the corner. Looked moorish somehow, I don't know why it should have, there was a big cross on top of one of the turrets.

The recreation hall was very large. There was a stage up front, with a record player sitting on a folding card table. A young priest was in charge of picking the songs. There were two big speakers, one on either side of the stage. If ever there was a lecture or anything, they would set up these wooden folding chairs. But for the Friday night dances, the chairs were pushed back along the walls, so that when you weren't dancing, you could sit. Mostly, it was the girls who sat, waiting for guys to come ask them to dance. The guys all stood around in small clusters, mustering courage to go ask the girls.

I remember the song they were playing that night.

This was forty-two years ago, but I still remember it. It was "I Can't Stop Loving You" by Ray Charles, a big hit that year. It was all about this guy who can't stop thinking of this girl he spent so many happy hours with. His heart is broken, you see. But he can't stop dreaming of her.

Girls don't know how long and how scary a room can seem when you're walking across it to ask someone to dance. Alicia was sitting with two of her girlfriends at the very farthest end of the room, her legs crossed, she was wearing a yellow dress, kind of ruffled, her legs crossed, jiggling her foot, she had such gorgeous legs, I loved her to death. The room was so long, Ray Charles singing about lonesome times, Alicia with her hair long and blonde, thirteen years old, Ray Charles singing about dreams of yesterday, Alicia laughing, looking beautiful, I stopped in front of her, the laughter stopped. I held out my hand to her.

"Would you care to dance?" I said.

I can't stop wanting you.

Alicia looked up at me.

"Get lost, faggot," she said.

"Let me get this straight, okay?" Carella said. "You *killed* Alicia Hendricks because she wouldn't *dance* with you . . ."

"Yes."

". . . when you were *fourteen*?"

"She called me a faggot!"

He was still Chuck at eighteen when a high school teacher refused to give him the A that would have kept him out of the army . . .

"But you promised . . ."

"Promises, promises," she said.

"You don't understand, Miss Langston . . ."

"Oh, yes, I understand quite well."

On the field outside, the football team was running plays. I could hear the coach shouting. A whistle blew. I had turned eighteen in September. If I didn't get into college . . .

"If you give me a C, it'll drag my average way down . . ."

"Then ask one of your other teachers for an A."

"Please, Miss Langston, the college will turn me down!"

"Apply to another college."

"You promised me an A. You said if I . . ."

"Oh, please don't be ridiculous, Chuck. I was joking and you know it."

"Miss Langston, please. Christine, pl . . ."

"Don't you dare *call me Christine!"*

Her words snapping on the air like the cold November itself. Her eyes glinting pale blue in the bleak grayness of the afternoon.

"They'll send me to Vietnam," I said.

"Pity," she said.

In the Army, he was Charlie . . .

"We called the enemy Charlie, too," he told them. "That was the name we had for them at the time. Charlie. That was my name, too, at the time. While I was in Nam . . ."

The girl couldn't have been more than nineteen.

I don't know why the sergeant thought she might be a spy.

It was a very sunny day.

I remember the sun was shining very brightly.

I was twenty years old, and riding in an open Jeep on a bumpy road with an automatic rifle in my lap and a girl with a baby hanging on to the hood for dear life.

You know . . . they teach you to kill.

That's the whole point of it.

You are trained to kill.

Even so . . .

The sergeant ordered her to put up her hands. This wasn't logical. He was grinning. Told her to put her hands up over her head. The Jeep was bouncing along, she was hanging on to the baby, hanging on to the hood, how could she put up her hands?

"Put up your hands!" he yelled.

She couldn't understand a word of English. She maybe didn't even hear him, the wind, the sound of planes strafing the village, maybe she didn't even hear him.

"Get your hands up!" he yelled.

Grinning.

He turned to me.

"Blow her away," he said.

They teach you to kill, you know.

"Blow her off the fuckin hood!*" he yelled.*

By six fifteen, they felt they had everything they needed for a grand jury. But Andy Parker still wasn't satisfied.

"Why'd you wait all this time?" he asked.

"I don't know what you mean."

"Why'd you wait till now to go after them?"

"Time was running out."

"I don't follow."

"I couldn't let them get away with what they'd done to me. I had to get them before it was too late."

"You mean before they died natural deaths?" Parker asked, referring to the advanced ages of the vics, grinning when he asked the question.

"No," Purcell said. "Before the cancer killed me."

"Pancreatic cancer.

"Was what I had.

"The chemotherapy was Gemzar and Taxotere. It was the Taxotere that caused me to lose my hair. It's only supposed to do that in eighty percent of the cases, but look at me. They told me my hair would grow back in six months. When we stopped the chemotherapy. Taxotere's a synthetic now, but it originally came from the leaves of the yew tree. That sounds medieval, doesn't it? Like doctors using leeches and such? Well, cancer, they're really just guessing. But the recipe, the cocktail, whatever you want to call it, the mix of poisons, seemed to be helping, the tumors in the pancreas seemed to be shrinking. Then . . ."

He hesitated.

The video camera was full on his face.

"Then in May, the middle of May it was, we got the results of the next CAT scan, and . . . it had spread everywhere. The cancer. Everywhere. The stomach, the liver, the lymph nodes, the lungs . . . just everywhere. The doctor told me I had potentially two months to live. That was the word he used. 'Potentially.'

"I decided to live it up in those next two months. Took out a home equity loan on my house, they gave me two hundred thousand dollars, let them take the house, who cares, I'll be dead. I recently leased a car, I'll be dead before the first payment is due, who cares? I'm making up for what I never achieved in my lifetime. Never accomplished. What I might have accomplished if only . . . if only people hadn't fiddled with me. So I decided to make them pay for what they'd done. The people who'd messed up my life. All of them. Do you understand? I killed them because they fiddled with my *life*!"

"You fiddled with theirs, too," Nellie said. "Big time."

"Good. They deserved it."

"Sure, good," Nellie said, and nodded. "You won't think it's so good when they inject that valium in your vein."

"That'll never happen," Purcell said. "I'll be dead before then. By my count, I've got no more than a week. So who cares?"

"Your fiancée might care," Nellie said.

Which was the only time any emotion crossed his face.

It was 6:43 A.M. when the video guy wrapped up his equipment and told Nellie and the detectives he was on his way. By then, Charles Purcell was already on his way to the Men's House of Detention downtown, for arraignment when the criminal courts opened. The video guy, who'd been interested in nothing more than the whodunit aspect of the case—this was, after all, merely a video, right?—could now pack up and go home.

For that matter, so could everyone else.

11.

When she opened the door at seven thirty that Tuesday morning, Paula Wellington was still in pajamas, her white hair loose around her face, no makeup. She looked fifty-one. She looked beautiful. She yawned, blinked out into the hallway at him.

"Little early, isn't it?" she said.

"I've been up all night," Hawes said.

"Come in," she said.

She closed the door behind him, locked it.

"I'm exhausted," he said. "I thought I might just sleep on the couch or something."

"That's what you thought, I see."

"You think that might be all right? My just sleeping here?"

"I'm *still* asleep," she said. "But come," she said, and took his hand. "Then we'll see," she said.

If she was talking about the fragility of relationships, he knew all about those; he'd been there.

If she was telling him that life itself was at best tenuous, he knew that, too; he was a cop.

"Then we'll see," he agreed.

"What am I, some kind of criminal here?" April asked.

Just answer the question, Teddy signed.

"Dad? Do I need a lawyer here?"

Good ploy, Carella thought. Turn the innocent smile and wide eyes on Dear Old Dad, always worked before, should work now. Mr. and Mrs. America at the breakfast table with their darling, thirteen-year-old, average-American twins—except that one of them may have been smoking pot on her thirteenth birthday.

"Answer your mother's question," he said.

"I forget the question," April said, and grinned at Mark for approval. Mark kept spooning Cheerios into his mouth.

Were you smoking pot at Lorraine's party? Teddy signed.

"D-a-a-d, do I *really* have to answer that?"

Carella had been here before. Too many times before. During too many interrogations of too many criminals on too many nights in the same grubby squadroom. But this was his own breakfast table, on a bright sunny morning toward the end of June, and it was his own daughter doing the tap dancing. He knew the answer already. He had been here before.

"Everybody smokes a little pot," April said.

Wrong answer.

"April," Carella said, "answer your mother's question."

April sighed a heavy, soulful, rolling-of-the-eyes, tweener sigh.

"Yes," she said, "I took a few tokes . . ."

Tokes, he thought.

". . . on a joint, all right?"

Joint, he thought.

"Is that such a big deal?" April asked.

Yes, Teddy signed.

"Well, I'm sorry, but . . ."

It's a big deal.

"Only if you're . . ."

In this family, it's a big deal.

"You're grounded," Carella said.

"Come on, Dad! Every kid in the world . . ."

"Not my kids," he said.

I'll talk to Lorraine's mother, Teddy signed.

"You'll embarrass me to death!"

Good. Be embarrassed.

"Besides, she won't know what the hell you're saying. She doesn't know how to sign. Leave it alone, okay, Mom? Don't turn this into a friggin federal case!"

He had never struck one of his children in his life, and he did not slap April now, though he certainly was tempted. Instead, very calmly, he said, "This isn't a squadroom, watch your mouth. You're grounded till further notice."

"The Fourth of July is coming! There's a big party at . . ."

"You'll miss it."

"What am I supposed to tell Lorraine? Jee-sus Christ!"

"Mom and I will talk to her mother . . ."

"No, you won't!"

". . . explain what's going on."

"Promise me you won't!"

"We will, April."

"She'll kick you out of the house."

"Not if she's smart," Carella said.

"She won't believe . . ."

"We'll make it clear."

April threw down her napkin.

"Okay, so *be* a whistle-blower, go ahead!" she shouted. "Ground me forever, see if I care! If you think that's gonna stop . . ."

Listen to me! Teddy signed, and rose suddenly, and pointed her finger at her daughter. *This is the* end *of this, have you got that? You will never again go anywhere* near *that shit!*

This was the first time April had ever seen such fire in her mother's eyes, the first time she had ever heard her use the word "shit." She hoped for a moment her father might change his mind, come to her rescue at last, thought at least her twin brother might say a word in her defense. But no, the censure at this table was unified and determined. No one here was about to enable her. She felt suddenly ashamed of herself.

She did not, however, say she was sorry.

"Gonna be a long summer, I guess," she said, and rose, and turned her back, and went to her room.

When they were small, if ever one of them was being scolded, the other twin would burst into tears.

Mark did not begin crying now.

"You okay?" Carella asked him.

"I feel like a rat."

"No," Carella said.

"Because, you know, she's right in a way. *All* the kids are smoking pot."

"You're not," Carella said.

Mark looked at him.

Then he simply nodded, and went back to his Cheerios.

Carella hoped he'd got it.

Kling still hadn't called either one of them.

By ten thirty that Tuesday morning, he'd caught two hours sleep, made himself a cup of coffee, paced the apartment for ten minutes or so, and still didn't know what he planned to do.

As it turned out, he didn't have to do anything at all.

The two most recent women in his life had already made their own decisions.

Sadie Harris was the first to call.

"Hey, Bert," she said.

"Sadie?" he said. "Hi. I've been meaning to call you."

"Actually, I'm glad you didn't," she said. "You were right, Bert."

"I was?"

"I'm not a librarian."

"You're not?"

"I'm a hooker, Bert, you were right."

"If you're kidding me . . ."

"No, no, cross my heart, hope to die. I was lying about everything but my name, Bert. You got a free ride cause you're so damn cute, be grateful. But given the circumstances . . . me black, you white . . . me hooker, you cop . . . me Jane, you Tarzan . . . I don't think we should see each other again."

"Well, I'm not so sure . . ."

"I am, Bert. Too risky, emotionally, and every other which way. So . . . have a nice week, be careful on the job, and don't go picking up strange girls in bars no more. By the way, I don't have anything you need to worry about. Good-bye, Bert," she said, and hung up.

Sharyn called five minutes later.

"I hope I'm not waking you, Bert," she said.

"No, I've been up. In fact, I was just about to . . ."

"I've given this a lot of thought," she said without preamble. "I know you think this was a simple misunderstanding, Bert, but I think it goes far beyond that. I think it goes to the very essence of our relationship. You followed me because you didn't trust me, Bert . . ."

"I was mistaken, I admit that. I'm sorry for what I . . ."

"It's not a matter of being mistaken, Bert, we both *know* you were mistaken. It's that you simply didn't trust me. And you didn't trust me because I'm black."

"No."

"Yes. That's what I think and that's what I can't get past, Bert. You didn't trust me because I'm black. That's what's wrong here. And maybe that's what's wrong with America, too, but I don't give a damn about what's wrong with America. All I care about is how this affects me personally. I know I can't live with it, Bert."

The phone went silent.

"You remember what we said after the first time we made love, Bert?"

"Yes, I remember."

"I said, 'Let's give it an honest shot . . .'"

"And I said, 'Let's.'"

"Bert," she said, and her voice caught. "You didn't," she said, and hung up.

12.

At 11:05 on Sunday morning, the Fourth of July, Patricia Gomez rang the doorbell to Ollie's apartment. She was wearing blue jeans, a white cotton blouse, and red sneakers, and she looked somewhat like a patriotic schoolgirl.

Ollie opened the door.

He honestly didn't know whether the smile on his face was an anticipatory leer or just a happy welcoming grin.

"Hey, Patricia," he said, "come on in."